Lock Down Publications and Ca$h
Presents

GET IT IN SLUGS 2

Family Over Everything

Written By

B. STALL

First Edition 2025

Printed in the United States of America

Lock Down Publications
P.O. Box 944
Stockbridge, GA 30281
www.lockdownpublications.com

Like our page on Facebook: Lock Down Publications
www.facebook.com/lockdownpublications.ldp

Stay Connected with Us!

Text **LOCKDOWN** to 22828 to stay up-to-date with new releases, sneak peaks, contests and more…

Like our page on Facebook:
Lock Down Publications

Join Lock Down Publications/The New Era Reading Group

Visit our website:
www.lockdownpublications.com

Follow us on Instagram:
Lock Down Publications

Email Us: We want to hear from you!

Renee, Looking Down From Above

I've been dead for days now, but it's like a part of me never left. Never took my protective eyes off my sons, Jason and Jaylen. Never left the familiar streets of Dallas that we all called home. I know I should be fully immersed in this Heavenly Paradise. Granted, I'm witnessing this splendor, thinking back on how many times I cheated on my taxes. But my God is a forgiver. He's healed me of my emotional and physical wounds and showed me that I've only been experiencing a fraction of what real joy is. That's why I'm so ashamed to even tell y'all that I brought some of my worldly ways with me. And don't go shaking your heads at me, thinking about how you can do better. I'm just a parent. A concerned one at that and I'm worried about my babies.

As y'all know, I was shot by those coward ass Golliday Boyz in the kitchen of my own home. Tossed and discarded like an animal on the side of the road. It was all upsetting. I was upset that I was taken away from them so soon, that I helplessly watched as they mourned for me and I wasn't there to console them. My death hit the family hard. But I never got upset with Jason though. I actually thought his trying to move us out the hood was quite noble. He may have gone about it the wrong way, robbing people. Though it shows the person I know him to be at heart. You know what, thinking back, I'm not even upset I got shot. I would rather it'd been me at the house that day instead of Jaylen. Those savages were determined to get at the family somehow and luckily that day, my death sufficed.

4

But now this nut PG has given Jason an ultimatum… give back all his money or pick plots to bury him and Jaylen. Then PG had the nerve to say he was gon' start with Jaylen first. I mean, really? You gon' start with him? You gon' kill my lil star before he lives out his NFL destiny?

Ooh, this is not good. Not good at all. If I had hands, I'd be fanning myself right now. Feet I'll be pacing. This ultimatum has my oldest stuck between a rock and a hard place. He has to tame the beast inside him to ensure the safety of his baby brother. I hope he does so. But I'm starting to adopt his attitude when it comes to protecting him. Though, there's certain things you just don't wish for from a place like this. So, I'll just pray and leave it in God's hands. A pause ensued as she took a second to do just that. In the meantime, I'ma be with y'all every step of the way. And don't worry about lil ol me, they can't kill me again~

Chapter 1

Bomp! Bomp!

Other cars' horns blew as 200 jumped lanes in his Tahoe, seeing the green exit sign near Coach Phil's estate. He was driving more reckless than Evel Knievel, spurred by the gunshot he heard that ended his call with Jaylen. The haunting blast threatened to fill his racing mind until he closed his tattooed eyelids and shook the thought aside. *What the hell was going on?* he thought. He and PG were supposed to have an agreement. One where PG got his stolen commas back and 200 didn't have to watch his talented brother get buried.

Just a few hours ago, the jack boy and kingpin came to a contentious understanding, with 200 leaving the impromptu meeting feeling like he was playin' with a couple weeks. But the clouds had barely darkened, and PG was already hittin' back, coming out of left field with an encrypted threat that he sent to 200's phone. It was a picture of Jaylen at the barbershop, which raised questions about how he got it. And it was accompanied by a taunting text that read, "Do I really need the money?" Hell yeah, he did. Why wouldn't he need over a million in cash, unless he was just hellbent on making 200 suffer for his siblings' murders? The matter had 200 fretting if his brother was in danger, which led to him calling, which led to him now wondering if he was alive.

"Come the fuck on!" 200 banged the steering wheel, looking wildly for an out from the halted traffic. The black truck was bucking forward like a bull ready to run wild from its cage. And when the traffic light turned green, he rode someone's ass until they got out the way.

Gunning the Tahoe through the wealthy neighborhood, 200 sat the Draco atop his black Jordan gym shorts. He had rushed out the house in his playground hoop gear, even though it was cold enough outside to see your breath. Shit was far from straight. Normal sensibilities seemed to be frivolous. He found it hard to be worried 'bout the weather when his baby brother's life was in peril.

200 zipped past the dark squad car that squatted in the grass median. Evidently, he found it hard to be worried 'bout the police too. In passing, he noticed the radar gun the officer held up. *Fuck!* And he looked like he was coming this way. He looked at his hued dash and saw that he was going seven over the speed limit. It wasn't much. But in this historically intolerant neighborhood, he might as well had been doing a hun'done.

Another glance in his rearview and 200's heart began to race. The squad car was driving with more purpose, sifting through traffic like a hungry shark stalking its prey. He put his seatbelt on. Not to appease the officer. Red lights or not, he wasn't stopping for these hoes. The fuck he'd look like getting pulled over and ruining his chances of getting to Jaylen? It was a possibility. But if it jumped off, he knew what he had to do.

Perspiration began to form on his handsome brown skin as he came to a stop sign with the police riding his bumper. The car was close enough so that he could feel the heat from its beams. It felt like at any given moment he might tap his bumper. He waited patiently to enter traffic. Then he accelerated through with as much normalcy as he could muster. He didn't know what to expect when he pulled from the stop sign. But when the piercing light swept right, he breathed a sigh of relief.

In a sudden surge of adrenaline, 200 gradually mashed the gas until he was zipping by foreign cars on this stretch of road. Blurring in his peripheral were palatial mansions. Sights that he would normally soak up, being the finer things connoisseur that he claimed to be. But he just stared straight ahead, his face gravely solemn. His frown was hard as cement. Hell, he might've set a record for not blinking. It wasn't until five minutes later when a sign gloriously dubbed Hillside appeared in the reach of his headlights, that his face relaxed in relief.

200 hit the left blinker as he turned into the gated community, his beady eyes searching and wide with alert. He didn't see the normal lights that accompanied a crime scene. But that didn't necessarily mean that Jaylen was okay. He ascended further along the freshly paved hill, passing large lots with pompous homes, before screeching to a stop in front of Coach Phil's estate. The sound of wind whirling reminded him it was wintertime, but the Draco on his lap let him know it was time to heat shit up.

Quickly, he jumped out, making his way across the sprawling landscape, until he was standing in front of the imperial sized door. He was sure there was a doorbell, but he didn't see one. So, he grabbed the large brass knocker and began to go *ham*. Someone in the house would have to be deaf not to hear him. Or in the case he feared most for Jaylen, dead.

Weighing this propelled him around back, where he crept along the house with the silence and stealth of a cat burglar. This reminded him of his legendary licks with the squad. Only this time, he was one deep. And what he was on the hunt for far exceeded dollar signs.

200 glanced around the grounds, looking to gain entry into the house, and saw light coming from the sliding glass doors. He ran to the door, thinking he might have to crack it in. But to his surprise, it slid right open. Toeing inside, he had his gun leveled like the law, on high alert, ready to put a nigga on a news reel at a moment's notice. The sight of his gun swept from the open kitchen to the dining room, until he

came upon the living room where Jaylen and his friend froze in shock.

"200!" They put their hands up. "What are you doing here?"

But 200 approached Jaylen with serious eyes. "Who's here?"

"Huh?"

200's brows narrowed. "Who the fuck's here?"

"Nobody, just me and Lil Craig." They looked at each other confused.

Sensing no danger, 200 secured his weapon inside his short's zip pocket. But he wasn't through with Jaylen in the least bit. He cut right to the chase.

"What was that loud bang I heard on the phone? Tell me the fuckin' truth!"

Jaylen tried to speak, but his words seemed stuck to his tongue.

"The truth," 200 reiterated before a lie left his lips.

"N-nothing," Jaylen stammered, avoiding eye contact.

"Oh, it was nothing?" 200 challenged, his voice stoked with cynicism. He nodded his head as if he was deep in thought. Then he surprised Jaylen with a two-piece, dead in his chest. *Bam. Bam.*

Jaylen dropped to his knees like his legs couldn't hold weight and began to gasp as if the room had suddenly run out of air. All he saw was 200's dark shoes as he stormed around him in circles.

"We got all this muthafuckin' shit going on. And you gon' look me in my face and tell me a lie?"

"I wasn't lying, bro. I swear." Jaylen coughed a few times to catch his breath. "We got excited when Lil Craig saw me on ESPN. And Craig's stupid self went and knocked over a vase. See, look." He didn't take him to see the vase. He took him to the TV. Craig grabbed a tablet-sized remote and pulled up the footage. As it started to load, smiles covered the boys' faces. The distinctive voice of an ESPN personality quickly filled the air.

. . . At number one, check out this move on the football field by the most hyped Texas prep star since Earl Campbell.

It showed Jaylen hitting a beautiful spin move, leaving a defender stuck like an Iverson crossover.

. . . Woop! Just leave him standing there. Looking confused. Looking for Mom. Somebody go and get this kid's cleats out the grass... The reel replayed in slow motion. *Jaylen, in his freshman year, set a state record for all-purpose yards in Texas. He's really going to be one to watch for. I bet the Longhorns can't wait for him to arrive on campus...*

Jaylen looked at 200 with vindication. "See?" As 200 picked up his pacing again, Jaylen continued to lay it on. "I know there's a lot going on. But you just a lil tight, bro. Calm down," he adamantly stressed.

200 continued to shake his head. He'd sent Jaylen to Coach Phil's as a safe haven. But the sound of the blast was so fresh in his mind that he was surprised to see Jaylen standing there. He knew what he heard, or at least he thought he did. But now thinking about Jaylen's reasoning, maybe he did need to calm down a bit.

His tight lips loosened. "That was a nice lil spin move." But then thinking about how an unwitting Jaylen was the main target of PG's vengeance, he made sure to stress, "All jokes aside, you gonna have to do better. I really thought something happened to you. Then you weren't answering the phone..."

Jaylen patted himself down, then seemingly remembered where he put it and removed the phone from the couch's cushion. "My bad, bro. I didn't even hear it ring."

"Maann, I oughta cave yo shit in one mo' time on GP. Bring yo lil knucklehead here." He gave him a hearty hug. "And don't scare me like that again." 200 didn't realize that he loved Jaylen more than he did himself. He wanted him to

10

live out his dreams. That's why he would do everything in his power to pay PG.

After 200 left, and Jaylen was sure that he was gone, he walked back over to Lil Craig and breathed a sigh.

"That was close."

"Who you telling?" Lil Craig raised his eyebrows.

Then they both went to the wall and removed a picture that was placed where Lil Craig mistakenly fired the gun.

"You think your dad is gonna notice that something is off when he gets back?"

"I don't see why he would. As long as I put this back in the drawer." He pulled out the expensive, pearl handled .38.

Jaylen was tempted to ask to hold it but thought better of it. "Man, if my brother would have seen all this, he woulda never let me stay here." He began to rub his chest.

"It hurt?" Lil Craig asked.

Jaylen shot him a condescending glare. "Why don't you let me punch you in yours, since you the reason why I got into all this mess?"

Chapter 2

200 saw drizzle in the headlights of his Tahoe. He was back on the road, driving with less purpose, but confused as to what PG meant by the threat.

Do I really need the money?

Combine that with the bang he heard and you might as well have said that PG had just killed Jaylen. He wasn't about to play this guessing game with PG any more. So, he picked up the phone to see where they stood. Instead of multiple rings, PG answered on the first go and his rude voice quickly filled the receiver.

"Yeah…"

"Yeah," 200 repeated. "Do you know who this is?"

"Of course I do. I could never forget the man who killed my only siblings."

200 hesitated before he spoke. They had a delicate situation. He couldn't afford to say anything to push PG over the edge.

"Man, what's up with the text? We was 'sposed to have an agreement."

"An agreement—yeah. We had something like that. I guess I was just texting my thoughts. I do that sometimes. Didn't mean to get yo lil panties all up in a bunch."

200 sighed and paused for a second to curb the venom on his tongue. Dealing with PG always stretched the limits of his patience. Dude just said what he felt, like his last name was Trump. "No, we *have* an agreement, not *had*. But you gon' have to give me a lil minute. I still gotta hit the streets and get it together."

"Can you get it together?" PG asked with uncertainty.

To 200, that was like asking if his name rang bells. He was an urban legend in the D. Their version of Pappy Mason. And behind Jaylen, he was gon' do whateva it took. "I can. But it ain't gon' happen overnight. I'ma need a lil mo' time to squeeze this money out the streets."

200 heard a concessive sigh leave PG's nose. Then after some deliberation, he spoke more sensibly. "Okay then, two weeks. Two weeks is what I'll give you to get that money together. After that, bro," he spoke as if they were cool, "I'm afraid I'll have to wash my hands."

"But two weeks?" 200 protested, "That's not giving me enough time. I'ma need more than that—"

"Two weeks is more than enough. It's a chance to save face. Something I didn't *have* to give. Fuck with me in two weeks."

200 insisted on common ground. "Remember, man, l ain't have nuthin' to do with that shit. One point two-five mil is a lot to come up with in such a short amount of time…" He wanted to continue, but felt the line grow cold. And when he looked at the screen, he saw the call had ended. But he sarcastically continued the conversation like he was still on the line. "So, maybe like four weeks would give me more breathing room. But no matter what, we gon' work it out."

Smacking his lips, 200 flipped the phone into the console. It never failed. PG always seemed to fry him out. *Ol' bitch ass nigga,* he fumed. *Talkin' all that bro shit like we like that. But I heard that part about I'ma have to wash my hands.* 200 wasn't aware that the truck started to reach higher speeds. But if he kept this up, he would be at his crib in no time. *What the fuck make you think you gon' lay a finger on mines? If anything, nigga fuck around and wash they hands with you.*

200 desperately wanted to dead PG and get stiff on these niggas and show 'em how a Highland Hills nigga do. But now was not the time to get temperamental. He had to be smart and rule his emotions, and not let his emotions rule him. The Golliday Boyz weren't slouches, and they had numbers. True to the old adage, there was strength in numbers. Even if twenty of them couldn't amount to one 200, the war wasn't worth him taking head on. It had already

proven too costly with the loss of his mother. And he owed it to her not to let the same happen to Jaylen.

200 let out a concessive sigh of his own. At least his day wasn't going as bad as when he thought Jaylen was dead. He was granted two weeks to come up with PG's stolen cash, and he found some light contentment in that. He spent the rest of the trip doing mental inventory of what he had in the stash. Then his thoughts deviated to how he was gon' come up with the rest. He was so far out there that it even surprised him to see the headlights of his Tahoe hitting off the garage of his home. A modern townhome in a good neighborhood, which he took the liberty of coining The Baby Ritz.

He reached down and unfastened his seatbelt, before idling the truck at the end of the property. Then after a breath where he took in his swanky digs, and the trees that secluded it, he hopped out and proceeded to the door. It seemed as if he was on the clock now. *Two weeks*, he thought. *Damn, it took me two months just to case Buck out.* He continued towards the property. He wasn't distracted by his worries for Jaylen, so he felt every drizzly splatter and gust of wind the winter clouds had to offer. This quickened his steps all the way to the door. But as he was trying to take out the key, he felt the cold press of steel to the back of his head. His hand fell to his side.

"Un-uh nigga," a voice growled. "This .44 will do damage, And I been meaning to hear how this bitch sound." He removed the Draco from 200's pocket. Then he pressed the *switch* deeper into 200's scalp. "Open the door... Nah, you don't hafta use ya key. Just twist the knob. It's already open."

Tentatively, 200 brought his right hand down and opened the door. When he shuttled inside, he was surprised to see PG sitting in his chair, surrounded by a brigade of unwelcoming faces, like he owned the place. PG was blowing his hot breath on 200's recently purchased pinky ring. Gone was the man who seemed sensible. From the look in his eyes, 200 could tell he was on some bullshit.

"You know, it's icy, but it's really not my look," PG held out the pinky ring. "Fuck it. I'll take it anyway."

200 was seeing red at the nigga before him with the thick bushy beard and distinct scar over his left eye. But he fought to reign it all in for Jaylen.

"Didn't I just talk to you? I thought you said two weeks."

"I did," PG gave off a devious smirk, "but that didn't mean that we can't get started today. Now, are you gonna come off that money you took of mine? Or should I do you like you did my sister?" He pulled a knife from his pocket and flipped it open. "Better yet... how 'bout I just do ya lil brother instead?"

200 looked up briefly and locked eyes with PG. In that short window, a myriad of encounters crossed his mind. He thought about how they found his mother and killed her. How they ended up with Jaylen's lost phone. The picture they texted of Jaylen at the barbershop, and even them getting his number and address. PG hadn't shown himself to be bluffing so far. 200 knew he meant business.

"Nah, playboy, ain't no need for all that. I told you I ain't have nuthin' to do with that. But y'all can have whatever I got here," 200 offered.

"Nigga, ain't nobody ask for yo life story," McGraw growled. "Just take us to the muthafuckin' stash!" He pressed the gun deeper into his scalp.

Even though his finger was just a slip of the trigger from going off, 200 remained surprisingly calm. He knew the game. In fact, he mastered it. And he wasn't 'bout to give this hitta any reason to feel like he had something to prove.

"You deaf or something, nigga?" McGraw nudged him a bit with the gun.

"Nah, I got you," His finger pointed ahead. "It's in the garage."

200 noticed the shadows of at least five men as he led them down to the garage, holding his hands above his head. His stash spots were fresh on his mind, because he had spent the bulk of the trip home thinking about them. He just didn't think he would have to come off the shit so soon. "I'ma need to move that shelf right there," he nodded. "It's a duffle bag hidden in the compartment under there."

"Nah, you ain't gotta move shit," McGraw barked. "Just tell us how to get inside the spot and we got you."

200 told them how to get in that stash spot, along with one inside his beloved Aston. And within minutes, they had everything laid out. "How much is that?"

"Six." 200's voice cracked as he cleared his throat. He shook his head, seeing the look of excitement on their faces.

Content, they rushed him back in the living room as if they had a trophy. And when they dropped the bags, PG had the same question. "How much is that?"

McGraw answered proudly, "Six hundred."

"Thousand?"

"Yep."

PG looked at 200 as he stood. "And it bet not be a penny short." He began to model the pinky ring, seeing how it looked on him. "Nah, you can keep this costume jewelry, it's too gaudy for me. You might need it to run the check up," he said, tossing it on the floor. But before he left, he stopped and gave 200 a stern warning. "As you can see, I can get to you or your family at any time. Try anything fly, and the boy dies."

Listening as the door closed, 200's nostrils seemed to blow steam. He massaged his forehead, but it couldn't stop his emotions from boiling over. "For Jaylen," he repeated, closing his eyes. "For Jaylen."

Chapter 3

200 reached back and grabbed his super thick down comforter, then flung it atop his head. He'd been laying in the darkened master bedroom for hours, trying to get some

rest. But his mind and body seemed on conflicting accords. "Fuck!" he groaned after dozing off momentarily, only to find himself back in a mental rut. This shit with PG and The Golliday Boyz had fried him out. He couldn't seem to get the image of PG's taunting smirk out of his head.

He stared at the ceiling for a minute, before tossing the comforter aside and putting his tattooed feet on the floor. It seemed he couldn't shake this funk long enough to get any rest. He tried smoking a phat doobie, and taking a shower, and right now he was desperate enough to start counting sheep. Frustrated, he sunk a hand into his knotted fade and somehow he wound up on his feet.

Looking back, he knew he did the best thing for Jaylen by controlling his temper and doing what they asked. But pretending like shit was all good was something his mind wouldn't allow him to do. These niggas had come in his home on some fuck shit and completely defiled his whole norm. It was like a pack of wild wolves had torn through, leaving behind a trail of devastation and destruction. Making a G like him contemplate only one thing—murder.

He started pacing, As frustrations rose inside him, an angry grumble left the corner of his mouth. "These niggas must not know that I'll put that hurtin' to 'em. Fo'real... fo'real. They wanna come in my house with this bullshit. They got me all the way fucked up." 200 remembered the smug look PG had on his face when he was flexin' with his new pinky ring. It was almost identical to the one Buck used to sport. Had him ready to put some new dimples right through his shit.

B'ough! B'ough!

"Yeah, nigga. What the fuck's so funny now?" he zoned out. He was no longer pacing in his bedroom. He was standing over a writhing PG. *"You thought that you could keep holding the weight of my brother over my head, huh?"* He fired a shot, intentionally landing mere inches from his waves. *"Haven't you heard that I was wanted for questioning*

in two double homicides? Or that I terrorized the city for close to two mil? But, I guess shit like that don't hold weight with you." He leveled the pistol over the distinct scar on his eye. He was out there bad. "*Well, let's see what this lil bitch right here do.*"

B'ough! B'ough! B'ough!

As 200 paced himself into a frenzy, he continued to slip deeper into a funk until a soft voice sprung in his head. *Don't be so hard on yourself. You did the right thing. You did it for Jaylen.* It was almost like his mother was talking to him. *Yeah, baby, don't let that temper get the best of you. Just do what you need to do to get you and your brother out of this mess.* His breathing started to relax, and he could feel himself settle down when he heard the vibration of the phone.

Bzzz! Bzzz!

He looked around before seeing the screen's glow beneath the comforter, then he slid his hand under the thick fabric and grabbed it. But upon recognizing the number on the text, his face formed a frown. It was the same weird ass number that PG had hit him from earlier. *What the fuck this bitch ass nigga want now?* he thought.

He opened the text, already on the defense about what he might see.

//: The money was short ... Dnt mk dat shit no habit ... R I'll cancel U & our lil agreement

The calm 200 felt had flipped like a coin.

"Short!" he snapped. "This bitch ass nigga playin' games. How 'bout I just cancel our lil agreement myself." He took off towards the closet and threw on some clothes and grabbed a unit. He was no longer in control, his temper had taken charge. "I know for a fact that money wasn't short. But if these niggas wanna keep playin' games, I got sumthin' for that ass."

19

Rushing through the living room, 200 grabbed a jacket and headed down into the garage. He couldn't say he didn't try *not* to kill PG. In fact, he had gone above and beyond. But it was like the nigga PG was just begging for a bullet. He was hoping he could give him some by the end of the night.

200 slid across the leather of his white two-door Aston. He knew that he would kill PG even if it led to cuffs. So, fuck it, might as well go out with a bang.

As the garage door ascended, he hit up Head to see if he was over at The Shack. He was actin' all scared when he mentioned The Golliday Boyz before. But he was hoping he wasn't on that tonight. Because he would hate to tie a comrade up. Luckily for 200, even though Head thought they would meet earlier in the day, Head told him The Shack was jumpin' as usual and he was welcome to come through. 200 made no mention about the rundown he needed about The Golliday Boyz. He figured it would be best to save that for when he pulled up.

200 whipped out the garage, turned up the Mo 3 on the radio, and brought his foreign engine to a hum until he was zoomin' up the interstate. The lyrics to "Outside" seemed to hit so close to home that he felt the song deep in his soul. Especially the part about "Until it hurts... It ain't no mercy..." He looked at the Glock extendo on his lap. He was about to bring some truth to that.

A beautiful hum left the engine as white lines blurred beneath him on the dark interstate. The roadway had probably never been this quiet. But it seemed all the noise was coming from inside his head. Rage blinded him from the consequences of what he was doing. He was locked in and ready to go to war. But dealing with The Golliday Boyz, he was sure to make Jaylen a casualty.

Just calm down, a soft voice said over his right shoulder.

Try anything fly and the boy dies, went a sinister voice over his left. 200 wasn't giving life to any of the voices in his head. All he wanted to hear was PG pleading and his gun going BANG!

A flash of lightning illuminated the quiet sky as he easily sped at ninety miles per hour. After making the race inspired dash climb a few more decibels, his phone blared with a ring and he didn't hesitate to answer. "What, nigga?" He thought it was PG.

"Wow. Did I catch you at a bad time?" Queen asked.

"Oh, my bad." 200 looked at the screen. "I thought you was this nigga who'd been playing on my phone."

"Sounds like whoeva this is has you riled up. I wasn't expecting to catch you like this. What are you doing?"

200 glanced at the gun on his lap. *What am I doing?* For the first time, he noticed how bad he was out there trippin'. Calling Head. Thinking about killing PG. He didn't even consider that Jaylen's well-being was at stake. *Damn, I'm 'bout to blow everything.* Queen's silky voice continued before he got a chance to answer.

"Mm-hmm. Mr. *What* nigga. You got me all in my feelings now. You gon' have to come through and make that up." Her playful vibe slowly chipped away at the ice around his heart. Even the speed on the dash started to decelerate.

"You want me to make that up? You sure?" 200 entertained her. He knew that if he didn't practically lock himself in the house with her, he would fuck around and kill PG, no questions asked. It boiled down to he could lay up under someone he was growing real fond of, or he could wind up doing something real foolish.

"Actually, I wanted you to come over here and eat."

"Eat?" 200 said in surprise, thinking something nasty.

"Yeah, I made my mother's famous blackened chicken fettucine. And it's a really big pot. I don't want it to go to waste."

200 looked at the time and saw that it was a quarter to twelve. *Fettucine at this time of night*, he thought, but he still

21

played along. "Iight, I'll be over there in a few. Start hookin' it up." After the call ended, he let out a conceding breath.

***

Knock! Knock! Knock!

"Coming," 200 heard Queen yell, and did a once-over of his casual black joggers and matching jacket.

He waited outside the newly built brick home, which hard work and a whole lot of parental affluence afforded her. While most people would have regarded the home as their crown achievement, the twenty-four-year-old hair care line upstart was already plotting on something more luxurious. She was ambitious like that. And fine like that too. She had that whole cute face, deep dimples, Lauren London thing goin'. Even a few months back, when 200 first shot his shot, he thought her style and looks reminded him of Nu-Nu. He could smell fruity scents as she approached the door. But when she opened it his eyebrows raised, thinking, *Damn.*

"What?" Queen asked.

"What you got on, that's what."

Queen had on some sexy satin boy shorts with peaches on them that seemed to be hiked all the way up in that pussy. The flirty baby tee she wore rose above her midriff, stopping right at the cup of her luscious breasts. Her dark hair was down, accenting her angelic features. If she chose, she could probably earn a living posting pics like this on the 'Gram. She smiled, showing cute dimples, then pulled him in the house and gave him a kiss. 200 gradually kissed her back then feigned disappointment.

"But what about the food? I'm hungry. I thought you called me over here to eat."

They kissed a few more seconds before Queen purred in the sexiest voice, "You wanna eat?"

200 answered with a barely audible, "Yeah." Then she lightly pushed him on the couch and straddled him, resting that hotbox right where it needed to be. As her soothing arms wrapped around his neck, she scooted her breasts in his face and looked in his eyes, permeating lust. "I got something in mind you might like a lil more than that." Since his mother's death, Queen knew he'd been in a deep funk and she was about to help him get his swagger right.

Queen helped him out of his jacket and shirt, then hungrily took a taste of what she absolutely adored, his bottom lip. She pulled away, then doubled back for another taste. Then she began to trail soft kisses along his chest down to the fuzz on his stomach, until her glossed lips rested right above the bulge in his joggers. Instead of freeing it, her manicured hands rubbed it, making it swell. The print alone made her lean over and kiss it, and somehow it snaked its way out on its own.

"Looks like somebody couldn't wait to see you."

A naughty giggle escaped Queen as she began to stroke him to life. "Is that right?" She then put the fat tip in her warm, saliva-filled mouth. After a few slow bobs, his stresses started to go away.

"Damn, that shit feel good," 200 half-groaned, half-whispered.

Queen whipped her fine hair over her shoulder, then began to show him just how good he could get it.

First, she started off slow and sensual, sucking his dick in circles and looking at him with those pretty eyes that made 200 shake his head. Queen was bad and she knew it. And she was on a mission right now, to take him out of the hell that he's been through and bring him heaven right here on earth. She began to slide that supa head up and down his pole, slurping as she went, and going even faster when 200 reached behind her and squished two fingers inside her wetness. It seemed his expert touch was distracting her from

23

her mission. But after a few moans of pleasure, she started to go even harder.

Removing her hands, she did her thing as saliva escaped the corners of her mouth. Then by the time she came back up, she had polished him all clean. She kept repeating this trick, much to 200's pleasure. It was just like the Nicki Minaj song said, "Wax on... wax off... Wax on... ˉwax off..."

The sounds of 200's toes cracking filled the air.

"Got damn, ma. You gonna have to slow down a lil bit. You gon' have a nigga bussin' after five... ten minutes."

But Queen didn't listen. And neither did 200's dick which he prided himself in having supreme control of. His soldiers burst forward like she had a vacuum made by Hoover at the back of her throat. The sound of slurping grew more fervent. She would have put Superhead to shame.

"Hold on," 200 protested, bracing her head slightly. If she kept this up, he was liable to catch a Charley horse. "Girl, hold on," he reiterated, scooting back.

Seeing 200's exhilarated expression, a laugh of pride left Queen. After sucking him dry, she had finally slowed down. She began to stroke his now semi-hard dick.

"I never did that before," she smiled shyly, referring to her trick. She wasn't sure if she did a good job, but she really needed to have someone draw up a copyright for that shit.

"Neva?" 200 repeated. Then after a long pause he added, "Well, you sho 'n the fuck did a good job."

Feeling like 200 didn't believe her, Queen huffed and pouted. "I'm serious, I hadn't."

200 accepted the truth swimming in her angel brown eyes and decided to compliment her skills. "Well, you did that like you had something to prove. What was you tryna do to me?"

"Tryna make you mine," she said sweetly.

Although 200 knew he was knee-deep in some beef shit and had murder charges looming, it was in his nature to entertain this chemistry. He pulled her closer by her heart-shaped hips, then looked in her eyes, making their spirits get in tune. "Oh, yeah?"

"Maybe." Queen's dimples turned flush.

"I like the sound of that," 200 eased off the couch.

"I like the sound of that too."

200 slid his hands inside her boy shorts then slid them down with gentle finesse. Her perfect peach appeared before him, and after licking his lips, he dove right in for a taste. A moan escaped Queen as he kissed her southern lips with the same comfort and passion as he did her other ones. She tasted good as hell too. It was like she took some of her cherry-flavored lip gloss and rubbed it right on that pussy.

He began to go hard, trying to get his get-back, sucking on her clit as if it was one of her erect nipples. He wanted to go "Under," like that Pleasure P song said, but he only got five minutes of fame before she stood him up and pushed him back on the couch.

Hastily, Queen brought her baby tee over her head then tossed it to the floor, exposing her titties. Now she had turned the tables and made this the Queen show again. And she was looking too good for him to put up any protest. Climbing atop him, she grabbed his leaning tower, then sank down on it as her eyes closed in pleasure. She began to groove at her own speed until she grew comfortable. Then, as 200 grabbed her ass, she started to pick up the pace. "Mmm!" she moaned as yummy sounds left both sets of her lips.

Their session was moving beyond passionate. She was in rare form. Her hands swept around him as she dug into his scalp and let her slippery wet tongue fill the inside of his ear. The zeal she showed was comparable to a groupie being with their favorite entertainer. And there was no holding back when it came to how he could get it.

"Got damn, baby. You riding that dick, ain't you?" 200 groaned.

"Mm-hmm," Queen nodded. "And it sounds like she talking to you."

200 was meeting her soft ass with aggressive strokes. "Oh, yeah?" He pumped even harder. "What she saying?"

"She saying that this dick good! Ahhh! And I think she 'bout to come! Oh, keep doing that shit. Yeah.... just like that."

They spent the next few minutes driving each other crazy. 200 was gripping her ass cheeks as he forced that dick inside her. And she was screaming at the top of her lungs, telling him how good it was. Finally, her love came rushing down like a faucet as she leaked on him and all over the furniture. Queen was starting to slow down, she was spent. But she had already awakened the savage in him.

"Get up," 200 told her as he eased her onto the couch. He attacked her already sensitive clit, before getting an idea. Placing her forearms on the carpet, he guided her lower body to the edge of the couch so he could hit it doggy style, just like that. As he positioned his legs so he was standing over her, he looked down at her goodies and shook his head. Picasso couldn't have painted a better picture. Pretty parts were in front of him. He was about to go ham. He tapped his dick all over her treasure before plunging deep inside. She was still sloppy wet and stupid gushy.

"Ohh! Fuck! Damn, Jason," she panted as he plowed on. Lil mama had nowhere to run, and that pussy was his for the taking. He kept dropping that hammer harder and faster, loving the control he had over that slim-thick frame.

After ten minutes of watching himself slide in and out of her, he figured he would try one of the other positions he had in mind. But just like that head, that pussy threw a wrench in his plans. "Baby, I finna bust. Shit!" He was holding off this nut with all he had. Then he realized that he couldn't escape the inevitable and started to go for broke. Pounding inside Queen, her moans reached a fever high pitch. He let off for a full minute strong before stepping out of the pussy and collapsing on the couch.

Feeling compelled to go the extra mile, Queen hustled over to his limp dick and began to lift him back up with no hands. She had his dick coated with saliva, which made 200 dig in the coarse knots atop his head.

"What?" she asked, stroking him. "I thought you may have had some more love left. I just wanted to make sure it was all gone." She gave it a kiss goodbye then stood to her feet.

After saying that she was going to get herself together and to grab his food, she showed him a half of a blunt that he left the last time he was over there. "You already know where the remote is... make yourself at home."

Queen took off through the halls of the trendy home. After spending a few minutes in the bathroom, she made her way down to the kitchen. She added a small sample of spices to his food. "He's gonna love this," she said. But when she walked back into the living room, he was sleeping like a baby. She laughed a little at his snoring then hurried to grab a phone to snap a picture for bragging rights. She was gon' have a picture to show 200 how she put that pussy on him. But at least the stressed-out jack boy finally got some sleep.

Chapter 4

Monte placed a tall can of Budweiser on the gas station counter, along with a fifty-spot to cover a box of 'Rillos and some gas.

"You must not be from round here, are you?" asked the pretty white cashier, throwing him for a loop.

Monte looked over his orange Burberry hoodie and matching joggers. He was swagged a lil different from these Texas Boyz. But she said that like he was a *Bama* or something. "Actually, I'm not," he countered, by pointing to a tattoo on his neck of the Gateway Arch. "Why you say that?"

"Mm... because we're not allowed to start selling liquor until after 12:00. State law," she informed, looking at him with a harmless smile.

"What! No liquor 'til after 12:00? What part of the game is that? Now that's some Texas shit fo'real." He reeled in disbelief. "At the stores in the 'Lou, you can get liquor damn near twenty-four-seven. That's crazy. But iight, though. Just gimme them 'Rillos and put the rest on pump eight."

Leaving the store, Monte was still low-key trippin' on their law when he noticed two niggas walking aimlessly and eyeballing him. He gave the closest one a nod, making his plaits shift over his face. But it wasn't on friendly shit. It was more with a frown, silently saying, *Nigga, what's up?*

These fuck boyz steady muggin' like they see something sweet. He got riled up. *Don't make me pull this .40 and show y'all the real reason why I'm ducked off down here in Texas.*

He kept fuming for a second, he was like that. His temper was as wild and crazy his cousin 200's. *Then y'all got me out here... burying my auntie and shit. Don't make retribution for that get ahead of schedule.*

Just to plex, Monte reached in his black two-door Benz Coupe then turned Money Bagg Yo's "Wockesha" up, while he let the gas pump and gutted a blunt. As he was standing by the Missouri tags, twisting the gas up, a Mexican cutie came out the store and unconsciously curbed his animosity. *Okay... okay. Cute face. Light skin. And that ass looking loose in that velour*, he thought. His dark eyes glowed with lust. He had never been the shy type.

"Dang, why you let me walk in that store knowing they don't serve liquor 'til after noon?" he played. "You seen them out of state tags. You knew I wasn't from 'round here."

The cutie slowed down, turning flush with confusion. "I didn't." *With yo sexy self.* "I never even seen you out here." *And that I would've noticed.*

"Well, I don't believe you. I believe you tried to play me out. And, now you gotta find a way to make that up."

Her eyebrow shot up and her arms quickly folded across her chest. "And just how am I supposed to do that?"

***

"Not out there." Doonie smacked her lips like it was hard to believe what 200 had just said. She adjusted her dated purple housecoat over her homely frame, then hustled to the curtains of her modest Mesquite, Texas, home. Squinting outside she saw the warped aluminum fence, the neighborhood smoker looking for a yard to cut, and the skid marks where Monte's Benz was just parked. "Now where in the hell has this boy done disappeared to?" she asked, turning in her living room to face a sitting 200. "He ain't been down from St. Louis for a full day yet and already I'm feeling like he's finding trouble."

200 looked up from his mother's obituary that she called him over to approve. He was tempted to say, *You wasn't worried 'bout that when you sent Monte to stay with his dad's people ten years ago,* but he knew Monte was too much for his poor aunt to handle. He also knew his aunt had a good heart, and he loved her still.

"Aunt Doonie, relax. Monte ain't *Lil Monte* no more. What is he... twenty-one? I know he ain't been in Dallas for a minute. But he should be iight."

"Iight my ass. I feel he gon' be iight too. But it ain't him that I'm worried 'bout. It's someone that he might run into. He think he slick. Tryna hit me with the *yes ma'am* and *no*

29

ma'am like he a saint. He think yo auntie green, chile. But, I hear what he's up there doing. Can you believe that this nigga shot three people up top, then ran and brought his happy-go-lucky ass down here?"

"No shit," 200 said, just to keep her going. His aunt Doonie was something else. He knew she could talk. It kinda shot him out there to better days. There was a point in time when they all stayed together. Doonie, Renee, Monte, himself, and Jaylen. It was around the time that 200's father was jailed for murder. In fact, there was a picture on her spotless glass table top to commemorate it.

When the Wells sisters weren't working, they spent their free time laughing and drinking. Their late night sessions were legendary. He could see that they both got that sassiness honestly. Aside from maybe their fine grade of hair, that's where the resemblance stopped. Doonie looked much older than she was for her age. While his mother made people feel like they were in the presence of an ageless angel.

His angel.

200 looked at the obituary in his hand and it felt surreal, staring at his mom. This couldn't be his T-Lady, photoshopped inside a frame with the date and time for her funeral service beneath it. *Nah. Fuck nah*, he thought, shaking his head as he continued to process the picture before him. He stared at her familiar brown eyes, her fair skin, her lovely face.

It brought a host of fond memories back to him. The time she took him and Jaylen to Sea World in San Antonio. The moans she probably heard before opening his bedroom door and catching a girl in his room. Smells of her cooking. The picture of the home that 200 showed Jaylen he was gonna surprise her with. His eyes refocused on the obituary in his hand. *It was…* he accepted it. *Fuck, it was.*

As pain crept in his heart then went up to his face, 200 looked off from the picture to try to keep his composure. But it was becoming more difficult by the second. It was probably easier for a toddler not to tear up after receiving a shot from the doctor. He tilted his head to keep· the tears from falling. But when the wind hit his eyes, a lone tear trickled down. Luckily for him, Doonie went to take another glance out the curtains, which gave him enough time to take his jacket and wipe his face. Meanwhile, Doonie was still going strong like the Energizer Bunny. This time, she was speculating about how Monte got such an expensive car.

When Doonie turned, 200 wondered if she could see the shift in his emotion. If the grief that he felt was written on his face. If she couldn't see it now, then she damn sure would see it soon on the news. 200 was about to hold the whole city hostage, if that's what it took to make sure Jaylen didn't suffer the same fate. Speaking of which, his iPhone received a text. He had been up since early this morning, planting seeds for future plays. And now that diligence was starting to bear fruit.

He read the text.

//: Mickey D's

Suddenly, that inner beast started to surface again. 200 knew his potential vic wanted to meet there in North Park. He was so thirsty to get the ball rolling on that additional six hundred fifty thousand for PG, that he decided to call instead of text.

"'Scuse me, Auntie. This ain't gon' take but a second." He brought the phone to his ear. After the second ring, his vic answered, excited about an offer he couldn't refuse. "So, that's where you wanna meet?" 200 asked. "Iight. I'm finna get in motion. Gimme like an hour or two. I'ma call you when I'm on the way."

"You're leaving?" Doonie asked, seeing him stand.

"Yeah, Auntie. I gotta go take care of something real quick. The obituary is beautiful. Tell Monte I said what's up. And I'll see y'all at the funeral."

31

He kissed her on the cheek. And as he started out the door, thoughts of The Twinz and The Golliday Boyz ran through his mind. He had been sitting on rage for so long from those ordeals. Now it was time to let some of that loose.

Two Blocks Away

"Monte, you gon' have to hurry up," moaned the Mexican cutie, looking back. My man gets off in less than an hour. And it's gon' be hell if he comes home and catches you here."

Monte kept stroking long and hard. "Girl, shut up and take this dick. Good as this Texas pussy is, I might tell him he gotta pack his shit and leave."

Monte's stiff comment got her pussy even wetter. It was something about the way he didn't give a fuck that brought the thot buried in her to the surface. Her juices began to flow between her legs.

"Ooh... shit! I'm cummin'!"

Monte felt his soldiers surfacing too and he busted right in his condom. He fought all the way until his dick went soft, then slid up out of that good and gushy.

"Damn, ma, we gon' have to get up and do that again. Make a video for my IG." He pulled out his phone. "What was your name again?"

Chapter 5

"Come back this way," 200 said into the phone, flashing the headlights of his Tahoe to show Rio where he was parked. At the last minute, 200 told his vic that he didn't want to meet at the fast-food place he suggested. Claiming that being dirty at this police hot spot had him feeling like a sitting duck. So, on some slick shit, 200 asked if they could meet here instead. This quiet park, which was likely to stay that way since school was in session and winter was still in full swing.

"Oh, I see you," Rio responded, coming up the street in his blue Acura Legend with what appeared to be his chick on the passenger side.

I see he brought his bitch, 200 thought. That wasn't something he had anticipated, but fuck it. *Just as long as he brought that fifty bands too*. 200 had been fuckin' with Rio for the past year and his money was always good. They usually fucked with each other after one of 200's licks. 200 would sell him the dope or goods that he made off his plays for the low ski, and Rio would gladly take it off his hands. Right now, Rio was thirsty for the two bricks and the jewelry 200 had heisted—a blinged out ring and a Piguet watch 200 had intentionally mispronounced, "Piggot" like he was green to the brand.

200 knew Rio's greedy ass would figure that he was trying to say Audemars Piguet. He could see him salivating now about how he would probably make seventy-five to a hundred thousand off the watch alone. Greed would make people lose their logic. And 200 planned to use this to his advantage.

200 watched with the calm of a lion stalking its prey as Rio parked adjacent to him on the opposite side of the street. After a few words with his lady, Rio hopped out and 200 did the same, keeping his composure as only a seasoned jack boy like him could. He threw his hands in the air coolly. "What's up, hood?" he asked Rio.

"Shit... You the man with the plan, I'm tryna see what's up with you." Because of the way he brushed his waves and the overbite of his teeth, Rio reminded people of the New York rapper Raekwon.

The bristling wind blew his black and red jacket open, allowing 200 a chance to scope and see if he had any weapons.

200 leaned in and gave him a bro hug but made sure not to bump him with his. "You looking good. I see you got the wifey with you," He gassed.

Rio leaned forward, then spoke in an animated whisper. "She ain't the wifey. More like my lil' eater, but don't let her know I told you that," he confided.

"Well, she gon' be doing a lot of eating once she see you with this." 200 held up his sparkling pinky ring. The VVS was hittin' against the winter sun, sparkling almost the same way it did when PG held it in the air.

"Whooo!" Rio brought his fist to his mouth. "This bitch stupid. I can't wait to see what the watch and shit lookin' like—where it's at?

Bout to be in the trunk like you, 200 thought maliciously before countering, "Where it's at? Sheit, where the money at, nigga?"

Rio smacked his lips and said in all seriousness, "Now you know I got the loot. It's over there in the ride, right under my bitch's seat. Don't play me like that."

200 tried to laugh it off. "'Iight, nigga. I'm just checking. Sheit, you know how this shit go."

But evidently, Rio didn't. It was like he was putting the scent of blood on his clothes, but he was walking next to a shark. The two men proceeded to the back of the Tahoe with 200 glancing across the park at a peculiar looking Range Rover. He was alert for any and everything right now. Maybe his adrenaline had him a little paranoid. Shaking back to focus, 200 popped the Tahoe's hatch, then grabbed a designer bag and sat it in front of Rio. Rio didn't even recognize that all his friendliness had absconded. It was hidden behind a mask of familiarity and comfort.

Rio rubbed his hands together. "You know, Two. You gon' have to start taking me on some of dem licks you be poppin'."

"I have," 200 said, making Rio's face screw. "You on one right now." Before the words could register, 200 slid the '40 from his pocket and violently slapped Rio right in the eyebrow. Blood gushed onto the ground as expletives left his lips. But 200 tried to gain control over the situation before Rio could panic and fuck around and make somebody call the police. "You got two seconds to stand yo ass up and get to that car." He placed the pistol to the back of his waves. "One... two..."

"I'm going! I'm going! Just calm down, bro." He tried to look back before thinking better of it. "'I thought that we were better than that. Don't make a mistake you'll regret."

If this was an attempt to gain sympathy, it didn't register with 200. He grabbed a fistful of Rio's jacket, then quickly led him to the side of the car where his girlfriend sat. "Get out of the car, bitch," he demanded. The horror on her freckly face and bulge of her eyes told 200 she wasn't going to be a problem. She had her hands in the air and didn't even know it was okay to open the door. "I said, get out of the car, bitch." She could see the evil in his eyes and quickly did as he said. "Get the fuck on the ground!"

The girl had no qualms about laying on the cold concrete and dewy grass in her tight-fitting blue jeans and cute coat. But Rio hesitated one second too long. 200 wacked him with the pistol again. "Bitch ass nigga, you hard of hearing?" The violent wack sounded like a head hitting a door.

Rio stumbled to the ground. 200 wasted no time zip-tying their hands behind their backs. He went straight into the passenger side and reached up under the seat where Rio said it was; feeling for any type of bag. *Hit dice!* He felt a plastic bag then pulled it out and saw the stacks of money inside it. After slipping the bag in his sleeve, he hustled back over to the curb and kneeled over Rio. Rio closed his eyes in prayer, expecting a boom. But loud words reached his ears instead. "If I even hear that you spoke on this to anybody, I'll be coming to finish what I started. Are we clear?"

200 wasn't even talking to the girl, but they both answered in unison. "Yeah!"

200 knew he couldn't gun down everybody he jacked. More bodies would only bring more heat to the mission. And if this bag was on point like Rio said, he still had six hundred thousand to get.

Hopping in the truck, he quickly started it up. It made a slight screech as he whipped out the space, then he began to open that bitch up.

***

Detective Winters cut through people at the Dallas County Courthouse like he did in his old football days. His big frame was moving so briskly across the linoleum flooring that he loosened his dress shirt collar just to get some air. He closed in on who he'd been trying to catch, then flailed his arm to stop her from entering the elevator.

"Prosecutor." She barely looked up. "Ms. Zellers, excuse me. Before you get on the elevator, can I have a minute?"

The distinguished older white woman, who was a tad bit on the plus side, but had an ass that any man would appreciate, glanced at her gold watch. "Actually, I'm pressed right now. I'm scheduled to be in court within the hour,

which may last into the evening. And I still haven't eaten."
Ms. Zellers started to board the elevator before Detective
Winters lightly braced her. He was determined to get her to
hear him out and wouldn't take no for an answer.

"Ms. Zellers, this is a matter of grave importance. I'm
trying to get the most dangerous man in Dallas off the streets,
and you can help." His words hung in the air. People on the
elevator waited restlessly for Zellers to make up her mind.
Detective Winters did so as well. "Please ma'am, just a few
minutes," Detective Winters pleaded.

After her ass had been sufficiently kissed, she turned and
led him down the hallway to her comfortable office. Closing
the door behind her she said, "And you betta make this
quick." Her arms were folded across her suit jacket and her
attitude said she had started her mental clock.

"Okay, I've been building a case for close to a year on this
kid out of Highland Hills named Jason Goodwin. This kid is
far from your local hood. He's a master at his trade of
robbing and he's a person of interest right now in at least four
homicides—and that's just right now. Recently, I received an
anonymous tip that claimed Jason was indeed involved in the
murders of Jamel and JaMia Golliday. Turns out, the tip
came from one of Jason's associates. One LaDarius Pruitt,
aka Zilla. I guess he was trying to be slick, but you know, we
have the technology to bypass—"

"Detective, sorry to interrupt." She looked at her watch.
"But I told you I was pressed for time. What is it that you
need me to do?"

"At the moment, Jason is out on bond for gun possession.
I need you to either reassess his bond or push for a speedy
trial. Something that would quickly get him back in custody
where I can press him about these murders."

"Okay, I'm still not seeing exactly why this is supposed
to be relevant to me."

Umm… because it's your job to prosecute criminals, he
thought, but chose to implore some finesse. "First off,

Prosecutor, you're up for reelection and a conviction of this caliber will put your name in all the major headlines." Seeing her picture the possibility, he drove home his point. "Ma'am, I'm telling you, you can't buy this type of publicity."

"Okay. Well, you bet not be shittin' me, Winters." She squinted.

He licked his lips and shot a slug about their past sexual rendezvous. "Have I ever?"

Her green eyes softened.

"Okay. Give me a couple of days and I'll see what I can do." As she walked off, Detective Winters looked at her ass and thought about some of the things he had done to that.

* * *

200 had a mug like a thirsty New York nigga scoping a tourist as he scorched up the dark highway, leaving Head's house. He was mad things weren't working out as planned. Rio had hit him with the fifty-one fake and planted twelve thousand worth of counterfeit in the sack. So instead of fifty bands, he actually had thirty-eight. And now his plans weren't lining up fast enough. But the deadline to get the money was still ticking.

He let out a sigh strong enough to bring fog to the windshield of the Aston, then mulled over the words Head told him before he left, "Be patient and I'ma put something in motion for you." The same redundant shit his last running mate, Tasha, had told him. But it was like they weren't understanding he needed something to shake now!

A hum, reflective of the frustrations he was feeling, left the engine as the hued dash climbed to a hundred. It didn't help that he thought he saw the Twinz a bit earlier. His so-called Day Ones that tried to kill him over the one point two-five PG was threatening to kill Jaylen for. He wished that was them bitch ass niggas, 'cause he damn sure was gon' give their tall frames more bullets then they could handle.

He felt like the streets weren't fearing him enough. *Maybe if I turn up this terror game, I can make it understood.*

After driving for a minute and plotting on how he could just start runnin' down on niggas, a kindle of logic started to push its way through. Here he was with over six hundred thousand to get up, and he was plotting foolery like he was ready for sixty years. *Just calm down, my nigga*, he told himself. *I know you ready to make shit shake, but just try to be a little patient. Your peoples said that they was gonna come through, and after tomorrow you'll still have twelve days left.* He tried to convince himself that it was ample time, but in the back of his mind he knew it wasn't.

When he kind of calmed down, the thought of Queen entered his mind. Her presence worked like medicine for him last night when he saw her, so he decided to give her a call. He felt around the pistol in his hoodie and grabbed his smart phone. She answered after a few rings and her sweet hello let him know she was happy to receive his call.

"I need to see you," 200 told her.

"Jason, I don't know why you just won't bring some clothes over. It'll save you the hassle of running back and forth." If this was Queen's way to welcome him to stay with her, it sounded like music to his ears.

"Alright, Miss Lady. Lemme go grab a few things. And I'll be over there in a few."

Chapter 6

Gospel music has the ability to stir a soul, to awaken, or in the case of Renee's funeral, evoke mourning. It had been a long time since 200 heard this type of music, and he wished he was listening to it for any of the former two reasons.

200 sat in the first pew at Golden Gates Funeral Home, whispering into a defeated Jaylen's ear as the preacher delivered passionate words. "It's gon' be okay," he softly consoled Jaylen. But when he looked in front of him, he had to take a strengthening breath. A few feet away, there was Renee inside a mahogany coffin, dressed beautifully to her sister Doonie's approval. Her fine hair was in a bun and her face looked as if she'd gained a few pounds. But he and Jaylen both knew who she was. There was no mistaking it. No one could match her glow. Suddenly, Jaylen erupted in tears and looked at his brother in confusion.

"But she'll never get to see me play... She'll never see me again."

Doonie looked at 200 with her prevalent crow's feet and her slightly graying hair, holding out her arms. "Let 'em here. I got him, baby. I got him." She gave him one of those big grandmotherly hugs, allowing Jaylen to cry into her dark dress like it would absorb his pain. And seemingly it did. Minutes later, the preacher had turned the sorrow filled occasion into a celebration, something that only rare preachers could do. People started to stand as he spoke about *uplifting* and the choir brought his sermon home with a spirited rendition of "Happy Days."

200 stood in the snug black Valentino suit jacket he wore with a dark shirt and jeans instead of slacks. He began to clap his hands like a Sunday worshipper, until he heard a voice in his head say, *look back*. He turned over his right shoulder towards the exit and saw Sabrina coming in. He knew this was her with the oversized shades and dark lipstick. What gave it away was she was carrying a mini him. He paused like he'd seen a ghost. It had been a minute since he'd seen his baby mama and Lil Jason. And he was surprised that she

even showed up. He turned back to see Jaylen still in Aunt Doonie's clutches. He desperately wanted to go back and check on his family. But the procession was ending, and he didn't want to disturb the momentum.

Alright, thank you everybody," the preacher said dismissively after wrapping up a powerful thirty-minute sermon. "Everybody, remember, she's in a better place." The preacher searched the standing crowd. "Amen!"

The church repeated in unison, "Amen!"

200 shook a few hands, but the whole time he was pressed to see Sabrina. He began to look around like a kid who'd been separated from his parents, his desperation growing as he scanned the crowd. But when he found the pew by the exit where she was sitting, Sabrina was nowhere to be found. *Damn!*

A heavy hand met his shoulder out of nowhere. "Cuz, it's been a minute." Monte gave him a sly grin. "We gon' have to do some catching up."

***

The large screen on Monte's smartphone showed wild images from his heavily followed Instagram page. To him, it was the most lit page out. To one of his bosses, it was drawing unnecessary heat. He leaned against the trunk of his Benz and continued to check some of his past posts. He was so engrossed in the addictive site that he never heard the leaves crunch under 200's feet as he left Doonie's yard.

"Damn, boy. Er'body in the house keep asking 'bout you. I look outside and you over here in the cold. What you got goin' on?"

Monte had this one plait that always seemed to dangle over his right eye. He flipped it out the way then showed 200 the blunt he had in his clutches. "Shit, 'bout to fire up." Regardless of the strength 200 tried to project, Monte could see that his mother's death was getting to him. He tried to take his mind off that. "Here, fire that bad boy up." By the time 200 brought the stuffed blunt of OG to a flame, Monte had found one of his recent posts. "And check this out." He gave him the phone.

200 looked at the image and started to nod his head. Monte was kneeling in front of a Rolls Royce Cullinan with a designer book bag with what appeared to be a shitload of money.

"That's you?" 200 asked in surprise.

"Nah, that's the big homie, Shon's shit. I was down in Atlanta with him when he first copped it. But that ain't nothing, keep scrolling."

200 landed on an icon that invited him to press play. He did so and after a few seconds, a laugh unconsciously left his lips.

"Nigga, you outta control." Monte had a covered up choppa on his lap, while he rode in the backseat of another expensive whip, and he was high as fuck, looking in the camera talking that slick shit. Now 200 was willfully looking through the images on his own. The next one shot him out there. "Nah, y'all doin' it up right here fo' real."

Monte looked over his shoulder and saw a few exotic women twerkin' in front of the outdoor fireplace of a palatial mansion.

"What's this?" 200 asked.

"Oh, that's me and some of my Ruger Crew guys. We had rented a mansion down in Miami to bring in the kid's twenty-first birthday." When Monte saw a dude walking past the camera shielding his face, his smile fell to a frown faster than a dog that sensed bad vibes. "And that's one of my so-called bosses right there, Lil Ronnie. But if you ask me, the nigga in the way."

200 could sense some animosity. "Where that come from?"

Monte smacked his lips. "Man, that nigga be low-key hatin' on the kid. '*Don't post this, them people could be*

watching. Don't do that.' It's like he takes pride in putting a
nigga down, when he know like I know he really threatened
by a nigga's rise." Monte patted the shoulder of 200's suit
jacket and offered the blunt back before continuing, "Cuz,
you should see how all the Ruger Crew youngins fuck with
me. I'm tellin' you, it's like I'm the president and they my
Secret Service. And if a nigga even sneeze wrong, they gon'
be ready to get active." He began to massage his chin slyly.
"Cuz, what you need to do is come up top and help me bleed
this nigga."

"Up top? Me?" 200's eyes flashed unnaturally. "What
makes you think I'll be on some shit like that?"

"Come on, Cuz. You know Ma is more like my homegirl
than my actual Dukes. So, first chance she got, she told me
how you was out here jackin' shit and terrorizing the city.
That's when I peeped your steeze and thought, *Cuz is exactly
what I need. A real hitta that nobody knows who can dip in
and out of state and help me get this money.*" When Monte
saw 200 giving his plot an inch, he tried to take him the
whole mile. "And this ain't one of them fraudulent ass
hustlaz either, Lil Ronnie caked up. If I say he got real bread,
he got it. And I put that on my gang." Monte's eyes showed
intensity.

200 felt his fervor but was somewhat confused. "I'm
saying, if this yo' boss, then why you hyping me up to get at
him?"

Leaning against the whip, Monte exhaled as if he was
meditating, but there was a frown on his face that reflected
his thoughts. "Cuz, I can see it now. It's only a matter of time
before we clash. And one thing about me— I'ma go 'ag
when it comes down to me and mine." He dapped 200 with
his elbow then added, "Sheit, you play dirty like I do. Don't
tell me you wouldn't do the same." The slight nod of 200's
head confirmed his thoughts. "Besides, with him out the
way, I'm next up for that boss spot. The person who really
deserves it."

200 knew he was in the presence of a young savage. For a moment, Monte had him gassed until the thought of his mother made him take umbrage at his own thirst. He looked around at all the cars that had gathered at Doonie's in remembrance of his mother. It was still hard to accept that this had actually happened. Fuck robbing a nigga, he felt like he'd been robbed of his whole world.

"Fam, I'ma keep it one hunnid, my mind ain't even on that right now. I just buried my 'T. My bro in there goin' through it." He pulled out a nearly empty bottle of Rémy as he stared off listlessly. He was at a loss for words, but he managed to find a few. "I really can't even think straight."

Monte was glad he brought Renee up.

"I been meaning to ask you about Auntie. Cuz, I'm riding for the cause. All you gotta do is tell me who to put the stick to."

Feeling aligned like a team, 200 started to open up. He gave him an expurgated version of what happened, starting with The Twinz, but omitting the parts about his beef with The Golliday Boyz and the money he owed PG. He downed the last lil' corner that he had in the pint of Rémy then pulled out another one and extended it to Monte. "You wanna hit this?"

* * *

To delete this message, please press 1 or hang up. If you'd like to replay this message, press 9 now, said Sabrina's voicemail. She was slouched over the desk inside the dim sitting room at her new loft. Normally, this is where she would get focused and get on her college studies. But right now, she couldn't even get herself together. The French tip of her nail hovered over the glowing phone's screen as the operator repeated the same monotone instructions. She stared off listlessly with sullen eyes for a moment before finally deciding to press repeat. It was the third time she had done so in a row. "It's all good, Sabrina. You ain't gotta pick up," 200 said with a heavy slur. "Just listen."

Clutching a tissue, Sabrina nodded as if he was right there. Then she shifted her frame in her lil' pjs to get more comfortable in the chair.

"Baby, look, I know it's been some bullshit between us, some animosity or whateva the case. But understand that there was never a point that I ever looked down on you for your decisions. You was right not to take shit from me or no nigga. But don't ever think that I didn't love you."

The phone went quiet for a second, before it was filled with the sound of 200 taking a sip. If it was true that liquor brought the truth out of people, then his words were pouring straight from the bottle.

"But I'ma be real with you, Sabrina. It fucked me up when you completely cut me off. Not being able to see you or my Jr. Or come home 'cause you had changed the locks— that hurt fo' real. I thought that we would weather any storm. But that's my fault, Brina. Blame me…" The sound of him turning the bottle up and guzzling again could be heard before he continued, "Blame me for everything. I was just too fuckin' embarrassed to tell you the truth. I mean, how could I tell my girl that I went and fucked off the money she gave me from her grandma's settlement? A hundred fifty K, at that!" He sounded truly sorry. "I couldn't bring myself to do it. So, I stayed away, hoping I could build everything back up," he distorted the truth.

But to a woman who had longed for answers, his words sounded like gospel. Here she was thinking he was MIA, because he didn't care. But it was clear from the emotion in his tone that the whole time he actually did.

"I guess I was just afraid to lose your respect. But as you saw today, the world didn't revolve around that incident. There are plenty of things that are more important than money. And family is one of them." When he spoke again, his words sobered with clarity. "Baby, if I never told you I'm

45

sorry before, I'm sorry for not being there for you and our son. And for not being the man you expected me to be. But I never stopped loving y'all and never will. It's family over everything. Damn, I miss y'all like crazy! And to be honest with you, Sabrina, I'm already missing Mama."

When the message ended, Sabrina's beauty fell to pieces faster than broken glass as her hands fell from her tear-stained face to the tiny bump burgeoning inside her stomach. It was an unconscious gesture to the great guilt she felt. A tremendous weight she would now carry with her for the rest of her life. When she first told PG, the unborn child's father, what the police suspected her firstborn's father of, she called herself getting back at 200 for playing with her emotions and bruising her heart. She never thought that things would play out the way they did. And although PG adamantly denied being involved in Renee's murder, she wasn't sure if she believed him. That's the part that made her feel complicit in all of this.

Feeling an abrupt queasiness, she jolted from the chair then ran to the bathroom as she started to vomit. She used her hand as a stopper to try to keep the vomit down, but some caught her white throw rug before she made it to the toilet. For a full minute, she heaved, throwing up like she was drunk. When it finally subsided, her thoughts went back to sweet Renee. "What did I do? What did I do?" she cried.

Chapter 7

"Any progress?" Slick asked, sticking his head inside PG's office at his dilapidated but profitable pallet recycling business. Slick was referring to the money they demanded from 200. His presence killed the loud chatter like a parent entering the room.

Their two most trusted henchmen, McGraw and Whitey, recognized this as their cue to leave, knowing that if Slick showed up, it was time for the Golliday bosses to get down to business. "Iight, PG." Whitey turned to Slick. "Unk." McGraw patted Slick on the shoulder, sending his pleasant cologne on an excursion around the room. The door clanked shut behind them.

"Nephew," Slick called to the crown of PG's head. "I see you all into that phone. What you over there doing?"

"Texting 200 another picture of Jaylen. I had a few of the goons follow him from school. 200 gon' really trip out when he sees this."

Either that or we will if you don't stop this nonsense. Slick thought. He usually possessed this Terrance Howard-*esque* mystique, but PG's comment had dampened his cool. He felt like PG had taken this Jaylen shit too far. Yea, he understood that they had to apply pressure. In fact, it was his idea that they do it that way. But PG had deviated from the original plan. And Slick felt like money or no money, PG would kill the kid. He began to scratch the shiny salt and pepper hair that adorned his head. Like lobbying his colleagues at the Dallas precinct to sweep Renee's murder under the rug wasn't enough. PG wanted to go out and compound things by senselessly murdering America's biggest prep star. This set off frustration inside him like a firestorm, but he found a subtle way to bring it to PG's attention.

"You know, we should really shift our focus towards getting that other six hundred fifty thousand for the plug. This connection has been fortified since your father took that bullet for me. I don't want to soil things by making it seem like we can't live up to our end of the arrangement." He met PG's eyes with seriousness. "Trust me, Nephew, this guy has been doing this even longer than I have. He's not the type of person you want to stall when it comes to his money."

When people talked to PG, they usually talked with deference, not assertiveness. But unbeknownst to the people on the outside who thought Slick had gotten out the game years ago, PG was actually the figurehead, while Slick was still running the show. Their operation ran smoothly. PG handled all the street shit, while Slick smoothed out the politics related to it from his powerful position inside Internal Affairs.

But placating Slick was becoming old to PG. Either that, or he was getting too big for his britches. Because it was hard to tell if there was a hierarchy when PG spoke. "Look, if you so worried about getting the plug paid, then you pay the other half. Because I ain't coming off another penny until I pull it out of 200's ass."

A jolt of anger hit Slick's eyes, and he was about to clap back. Then he saw an untimely smile spread across PG's face. Maybe the death of his lone siblings did make him a little crazy.

"And since you brought my father up, I've got some really good news. I mean, good news. You might even get excited when you hear this." PG sat his phone down and watched Slick's reaction to see if his words made a splash. "You know I been infatuated with the circumstances surrounding my father. So, I hired a private investigator to look into the murder. Not that I'm tryna solve some decades-old case or no shit like that. I really just want to learn who did it so I can deliver my own form of justice." He stared off listlessly until the prospect became real to him. "They thought they had gotten away with it. But the P.I. promised that if he could help it, they wouldn't. He said that he should be making some headway soon. So, what do you think?" He smiled.

"I think I better go and pay the plug before we have a war on our hands," Slick said matter-of-factly. "In the meantime, you get yo' head in the game. Let go of this wild goose hunt and get back focused on the money." Slick left out of the door hastily without looking back.

Chapter 8

200 stood in line at the famed hood restaurant, Sweet Georgia Brown on a chilly sun filled morning. The kitchen came to life with the clinking of spatulas and a plethora of aromas. Eggs, green peppers and onions, French toast, and just about every part of the pig that one could think of. But food was the furthest thing from 200's mind. The thirsty jack boy was more infatuated with the guy that stood two patrons in front of him.

200 watched with the glare of a hawk and the venom of a snake as his beady eyes didn't so much as blink. He scanned the stocky guy's blue work wear, all the way up to his orange snapback, paying special attention to the company's logo printed on the side of it. The logo was crucial. To everyone

else it meant nothing. To 200, it meant that he was that much closer to settling his debt with PG.

Earlier in the week, 200 got up with his lone soldier, Tasha. She quickly gave him the rundown about her homegirl who worked at the club where she danced. Tasha said her homegirl was trying to get back at her bitch ass ex, a man that was employed to fill up ATMs with cash, who practically made her drive to the clinic to get an abortion. *Fat head ass nigga*, she complained. Too bad he had broken the wrong girl's heart. Now, the girl was only concerned with getting her cut of the sixty thousand she put their squad on.

The vic moved to the counter and began to happily stare at the prearranged food. As he pointed at different items, wavering about his decision, 200 took this opportunity to look outside and into the smoker's rental that Tasha occupied. He asked with his eyes if everything was set. She gave him a subtle nod, which indicated the GPS tracking device had been placed on the vic's car.

200 looked back at him, desperately wanting to draw that toolie and force this clown nigga to get inside the trunk. But he just couldn't do it. Not right now, at least. It was still an hour before he started work, and 200 knew that's when he would have the money on him. As a small bell over the door announced the vic was leaving, 200 waited after one more person then made it to the front of the line.

"Lemme get a dark coffee with a lot of sugar and cream, please," he ordered.

"Coffee?" scoffed the cashier who bore this strange resemblance to Fred Sanford. "You sure you don't want none of this good food?"

"I just need to put a lil' something on my stomach. Long night," 200 responded. But that thirty inside his coat told him it was about to be an eventful day.

200's order was quickly filled, and he made his way out to the parking lot. Tasha sat up on the passenger seat with anticipation. She wasn't the dolled-up Tasha she normally was, but even in disguise she was still cute as fuck. She wore a maroon streaked sew-in atop her head. Sunglasses covered her kissable chocolate face. Even sitting down, one could tell that ass was poking out of them jeans. A nip entered the car as 200 hopped in.

"The GPS works good. He just left the lot, but he hasn't gone far." She showed him the screen.

As 200 backed out the parking spot, he glanced over at the moving red dot on Tasha's phone. It felt good to see the mouse headed for the trap. But his phone began to vibrate like crazy, making him lose focus.

"Let me grab this real quick," 200 said, reaching inside his skinnies. He sat comfortably, then got in traffic. The minute he opened the text on his phone, trepidation hit him in waves.

"What's wrong?" Tasha asked, seeing him with a death grip on the phone.

"Nothing," he lied, even though he couldn't escape the damning picture of Jaylen outside his school. "Let's just go get this money."

***

When Larry parked in the alley behind the 7-Eleven, he immediately felt flutters of nervous energy. He knew the dangers of bringing money like this to the hood. That's why even though his job didn't require it, he kept him a little .38. *I bet not come out to the 'Grove butt naked,* he thought. *These niggas out here coined the term, 'eatin' greedy.'*

Before Larry killed the engine of his white Toyota Corolla, he scrutinized the area for any blind spots where trouble might lurk, starting with the decaying wood fencing that separated the neighboring houses, on down to the far end of the alley where dope exchanged hands. He even looked by the green trash can where he swore one morning he saw a young trappa getting domed up by a crackhead that had a hard time keeping her wig on her head. It was all a part of him being serious about his job, which entailed one thing, making it to that gray steel door with the money. That gray steel door where he would do a special knock, and the manager would let him inside.

A sudden surge of courage rose inside him as he exited the car, looking every bit of a utility worker. It was all a part of his ruse. Far as he knew, everybody would think he was a meter reader, when he was actually toting enough money to put them all in the· game. He opened the back passenger door, where there was an aluminum cage his employer made all of their workers get installed. He then unlocked the cage and reached deep in the compartment for the tan suede security bags, holding what was presumed to be sixty thousand. But in doing so, he violated one of the company's golden rules, never leave yourself open.

A frightening object poked him in the ribs. "Gimme the bags," a masked up 200 demanded. "And if I waste one more breath, I'ma start puttin' these slugs in ya."

Larry gasped as a tidal wave of alarm washed over him. "H-here, homie. T-take this shit," he stuttered and stammered. "You can have all of this… just… please don't shoot me!" Although the pleas Larry was copping was right on time, the lackadaisical way he was moving wasn't.

"Bitch nigga, you playin' games. C'mon with them bags!" 200 looked up to make sure nobody was coming. As the first one touched his hand, 200 heard locks being opened at the gas station's back door. His mouth tightened as he sent a flurry of shots denting the door just to tell whoever was behind it to stay put. "Gimme that shit!" he snarled, snatching both bags out of Larry's hands. "And since you playin' games, you 'bout to regret playin' with a G!"

F'ough! … F'ough!

200 sent separate hollows to his back and hip. He didn't know why he did it, but it was too late to wonder now. He turned and peeled towards the end of the alley to see Tasha

rolling the smoker's rental to a stop. The door swung open, and he quickly hopped inside. In that millisecond it took for him to close the door, he saw the gleaming barrel of Larry's pistol aimed at the windshield. "Go!" 200 struck the dash as shots broke out.

They made it about four tire-screeching blocks, before Tasha broke the silence.

"Did you get it?" she asked, referring to the sixty racks.

"I think so. But you gon' have to tell yo' girl it wasn't as much as she said."

* * *

A part of 200 was still stuck in *go* mode but for the most part, he was relatively chill. That was, until they pulled into The Flats where Tasha resided, and saw a clique of young niggas that gave 200 a bad vibe.

"Park a lil' further down there." 200 pointed ahead. "We don't want the police seeing this hot ass car. And damn sho' not next to ours."

As Tasha solemnly obliged, 200 kept his squint zeroed in on the rowdy hardheads that loitered the premises as if they policed it. They looked young, but old enough to play with that toolie. They all wore shiesty glares. 200 didn't feel comfortable reaching down to grab the other security bag, so he slid it under the seat with his foot for now.

"Why you do that?" Tasha asked.

Stress showed in 200's reflection as he peered out the window, studying the lot.

"Y'ont see these niggas studying the car? They eyeing us like we the opps, and it's definitely more of them than I got bullets left in this gun."

"Boy, c'mon. This is *my* hood. Ain't nobody finna do nothing. Just make sure you stay close to me, and I'll have your back," she teased, tapping his leg before she got out.

200 spilled out behind her but kept his mug serious as he was welcomed to their hood with loud music and a heavy cloud of *loud* smoke. As they proceeded to Tasha's apartment, one of the hardheads wearing a Dickie's jumpsuit, hollered out to him to see if he wanted to buy some loud. "Nah, I'm good," he declined, looking over and seeing that their shiesty glares remained. Any other time he would have checked that shit, but right now he was just focused on getting safely inside with the money. Feeling the security bag slip, he quickly hustled up to Tasha and grabbed her by the waist, pressing himself into all that cushion.

A soft moan escaped her. "Okay, that's a surprise."

"Nah, this hoe ass bag was about to fall down my leg. Just go with it," he whispered softly into her neck. Like they couldn't get enough of each other, they entered the apartment, and when the door closed behind them, he allowed the bag to fall down his leg. "That was close," 200 said.

But it can get closer, Tasha thought, staring him down. Secretly, she'd always had a thing for 200, and their bodies touching had her hotter than a pie out of the oven. Watching him sit on the couch, she subtly licked her lips and became even more turned on by all of his thug essence. Those damn tattoos. His knotted hair. That handsome brown skin. *When you gon' stop playing, Jason Goodwin, and come get this pussy?*

"Look..." She took a light breath to curb her sexual impulses. "I'ma run upstairs and go take a shower. It should give you enough time to take care of that." Her eyes popped at the security bag in his lap, though the whole time she was really lusting 'bout that dick. She hung her jacket up, then began to toss her clothes aside like she was back in her element at Diamond Cabaret. Shoes, shirt, bra—they all fell in the same pile on the hardwood floor.

200 caught a good glimpse of her side boob and the parts of her butt that couldn't fit in them jeans as she scurried

upstairs. 200 shook his head. Tasha knew what she was doing and under any other circumstances, he would have given her what she wanted. Staying focused, he looked at the different appropriations of freshly printed bills. Large and small, with twenties being the most prevalent of the bunch. He thumbed through the money fast, then he reclined against the firm blue couch and blew a relaxing breath towards the living room's ceiling. This felt like a small victory of sorts. It had been a hectic past four days. Just thinking about that whirlwind had 200 unconsciously shaking his head. But with the twenty-nine racks he just counted, plus the other bag outside… he paused for a second. *Oh shit. The other bag.*

Forgetting about the leeway he was making, he ran to the blinds and peeked out to check on the car. He saw his black Tahoe, Tasha's dated Infiniti, and the smoker's rental a good ways away from the apartment. Far as he knew, everything looked kosher. Even the gang of hardheads had somewhat dispersed.

Feeling his worries wane, he went back and plopped on the couch, then finished handling his business. He knew Tasha's girl would question the five racks she gave her. But by the time Tasha finished calling her out about overhyping the money, he was sure her girl would gratefully take it. He slid her money across the glass table, as well as a matching stack for Tasha. Then he heard a beeping alert from the phone in his pocket.

When he opened the screen, it was just letting him know that his phone needed to be charged. But seeing that it was Tuesday, his thoughts immediately went to Jaylen.

"Damn, lil' bro's ceremony is today," 200 mumbled under his breath. He was referring to the prestigious annual football banquet where the Metroplex's top football player would be honored. For the North Texas elite, this was as big as it got. Professional studs like Myles Garrett and Kyler Murray had previously been bestowed the honor. It was a good indication that the recipient was NFL bound.

He picked up the phone to dial him up, and after a few rings, a whispering Jaylen answered. "What's up?"

"What's good, lil' bro? Why you whispering?" he mirrored Jaylen's tone.

"I'm here now at the Pavilion, suited and booted. And the ceremony is underway."

"Suited and booted?" 200 repeated, admiring his swag.

"No doubt. I'm on my black-tie affair *ish*, bro. I got the patent leather shoes. Fitted tux. You would think I was getting ready for the NFL draft or something. But look," Jaylen began to extenuate, "I'm in like the first few rows of tables. So, I'm kinda putting myself on blast." Some light applause rose before Jaylen spoke back in the phone. "Love you, bro. I gotta go. Here, talk to Coach Phil." He rushed off the phone.

Got damn, 200 thought. *Well, if it wasn't good ol' Coach Phil.* He had taken Jaylen under his wing since he'd been in high school and had been sheltering the phenom at his pompous estate for the past six days. During that time, PG and his squad had popped up at 200's crib and revved up the pressure to get his money. 200 couldn't have been more grateful that Jaylen wasn't staying there.

After hearing Coach say hello, 200 responded, "Coach Phil. Glad to hear you're finally back in town."

"Good to be back too. I'm normally not away from home for that long. But I was at a realty conference. Business. You know how that be."

"Yeah, I do. I'm pretty busy with some myself," 200 said, but his mind was focused on something about Coach Phil. There was a certain familiarity that he thought he recognized in his voice. But he was getting to know this particular trait about Coach Phil, that he always spoke as if he knew a person.

"So, what you gonna do?" Coach Phil asked. "You got a suit in that closet. You might miss the ceremony. But you can make it to the dinner banquet."

200 thought about the deadline to meet the quota. "Actually, I can't. To be honest, I probably be rippin' and runnin' for the next few days."

"Hold on," Coach Phil cut in early, "Don't mean to interrupt you, but Jaylen and the other guys are headed on stage." As tension filled the room, Coach whispered into the phone, "They're about to give out the Statesman award." A courteous round of applause rose, and the voice of the announcer followed. Then, after a moment of stillness, Coach Phil erupted like his favorite team had just scored a touchdown. "He did it! At fifteen. Your brother just did it. Jason, I'll talk to you later. I'm 'bout to join him on stage." He ended the call with the quickness.

200 smiled as if he had won the award himself. But it diluted a fraction when he thought he heard something break. Still, the sound didn't hold his attention long enough to register. His little brother was on his way. He was doing big things.

As he repositioned himself on the couch, a light screeching sound reached his ear. Followed by a more alarming one, then the gunning of an engine. It sounded suspicious. He ran to the blinds and peeked out the window. "Muthafucka!" His fist slammed into his palm. The smoker rental was gone. More importantly, so was the bag!

Tasha came rushing out of the shower with soap glistening on her naked body. "What's wrong?" she asked.

200 glared at her pussy before curbing the lust in his eyes.

"The car! A muthafucka done stole it!" he said, rushing out of the apartment with his gun in hand. *These lil' dirty ass niggas must not know who the fuck they fuckin' with.* 200 followed the deep tire marks all the way to the apartment's entrance. He looked from left to right of the city streets. *Bitch*, he fumed. The car was nowhere in sight.

Chapter 9

Two prominent Dallas attorneys were dining at a new upscale restaurant when their conversation reached a roadblock. "One year!" Daley said in rebuke, his grayish eyebrows furrowing. "Look, Zellers, I know my client. And there's no way he'd go for that."

A devious smirk rose on the prosecutor's ardent face as she observed 200's lawyer. While Daley seemed pressed, the matter didn't really move her. Taking her sweet time, she enjoyed a bite of her plant-based steak. She loved being in control. She was the definition of a pit bull in a skirt.

"Not only will he take it. But he'll be in court by next Thursday," Zellers said definitively, before flagging over the slender waiter for the bill.

Daly glanced at the platinum Rolex passed down to him by his father. Next Thursday was just a week away. He knew Zellers didn't call him to do lunch just to tell him this. "C'mon Shellie," he called her by her real name. "I thought our rapport was better. You said a year. I was thinking we could plead this down to probation."

Zellers chuckled at the exasperated look on his pale face. "You might want to go ahead and call him. Thursday's not that far away."

"Shellie, for Christ sakes!" Daley tossed his handkerchief near the china. It was hard to tell if he was more upset that he didn't get a better offer, or because he had to stop eating his well-seasoned food. He walked over to the bar to get some privacy, then reached in his black peacoat and fished out his phone. A few rings later, a lethargic 200 answered. Most of what came out of his mouth sounded garbled. "Mr. Goodwin, hi. How are you?" He listened until he felt 200 was coherent, then he continued. "Well, I'm sorry to wake you, but let me cut to the chase. I had a conference with the DA, and she won't go any lower than a year on the gun charge."

"A year! What do you mean *a year?*" 200's voice boomed. He was so loud that Daley took the phone away from his ear. "I ain't got no prior felonies. That's just a gun. You mean to tell me you can't get me probation?"

"Sorry, pal, she seems to be playing hardball on this one. I can't get her to budge an inch. And you're scheduled for court next Thursday."

200's voice blared so loud now it seemed to literally blow the attorney's wig back. Daley looked from his phone to the prosecutor, then back to his phone. The last thing he heard before 200 hung up was, "You gon' get me probation, ol' stupid ass nigga." With raised eyebrows, Daley returned to the table. His pale skin was now beet red.

"So, how'd it go?" Zellers teased.

"Let's just say not so well."

＊

After a much anticipated call about 200 from the DA, Detective Winters ended the call and clapped exuberantly. "Yes! That's what the fuck I'm talking 'bout!" Now it was time to do some questioning. "Can't wait to get his lil' nappy head ass in here to answer for all these murders."

Relaxing his husky frame on the seat of his tinted-out Ford Explorer, Detective Winters reached inside his wool suit jacket and brought a square to his dark lips. It was his version of a cigar. He had discovered over the years that his leverage was better when his targets were in custody, and he was practically salivating at another potential stab at 200.

The Newport that he fired up had barely come to a cherry when a teal Charger swooped in the parking spot adjacent to him. After a few nervous glances around the bustling shopping complex, a tall, brown-skinned man with a serious mug appeared, sporting a bushy beard. He quickly threw the fur-rimmed hood of his coat over his head. It wasn't the forty-degree breeze that instigated this, it was the fact that he didn't want anybody to see his face. He caught a reflection of himself blowing into his hands before he hopped inside the smoke-filled tan Explorer.

"Mr. Pruitt," Detective Winters acknowledged him, but the streets knew him as 200's former day-one, Zilla. "I've got some good news. The DA set 200's court date for next Thursday, and we should have him in custody and off the streets."

"You serious?" Zilla asked, zoning to a place of reflection. His whole reasoning for taking Detective Winters' advice and giving up his anonymity was so his tips about the Golliday murders would be taken more seriously. Not to mention, so he would have peace of mind that his family was out of harm's way, with 200 being in jail, of course. Zilla had hit enough licks with 200 to know the man was a lunatic. He had already been sighted several times outside of his baby mama's crib. *Fuck, I wish those bullets would have killed his ass.* "So, when you say, 'off the streets,' you mean for good?"

"Not quite yet. I like how you think. But not quite yet. He's scheduled to take a year in court. Then once he's in custody, I can grill him with this new information you gave me."

"That's good." Zilla breathed a sigh of relief.

"Good? No, that's great. I've been chasing 200 around like these white folks chase Sasquatch. And I'm excited as you are that he's about to be brought to justice. But remember," he turned serious, "he's not in custody just yet. I know you're ready for things to get back to normal, but if I were you, I'd play it safe."

"Will do," Zilla said. After receiving Detective Winter's assurance that they were no longer taping *The First 48* and he wouldn't appear in any episode, Zilla said his pleasantries and started out the door. His Polo boot was halfway on the pavement when he abruptly pulled it back. "Oh, shit!"

"What?" Detective Winters squinted, absorbing his angst.

Zilla shrunk further into the hood of his brown coat. "My twin just showed. Oh shit. I hope he don't see me."

"Your *who* just *what*?"

"My twin, he's parking his Range across the lot. Nah, don't look. Fuck! Man, we gotta shake this spot." Zilla was already in Shocka's doghouse because he wasn't with how he crossed 200. Now, if Shocka found out he was snitching, he would really be fucked up with him. Zilla saw his door open, and his fears amplified. "Just leave. Please. We can pull back up here later to get my car."

Detective Winters didn't want to breach the confidentiality of his informant, so he left the lot like he was being called to a scene.

Chapter 10

Head stepped inside the lavish penthouse recording studio and was taking in its luxurious layout when his eyes got stuck. Before him, laughing on the Italian white leather couch, is what Da Baby would call two masterpieces. The girls didn't notice the affect they were having on Head, but someone else did and playfully nudged his gargantuan frame.

"That's salt and pepper right there," Fooley Wayne whispered. "They spend so much time in this bitch that I'm feeling like charging 'em the standard ten K for a session. But what's good?" Fooley Wayne extended his hand, making his icy watch and bracelets glide from the cuff of his black Dior robe. The Oak Cliff rapper wasn't dressed for a show or a shoot. But rather the self-proclaimed King of Drip was just at the studio doin' him. He felt being dressed for the job helped him get in his zone. And as evidence of his wave, it was helping the twenty-three-year-old get to the bag. Well, that, and unquestionably his internet drama. The dread sporter who possessed the virility of a head *bussa* seemed to wake up to beef as easily as someone woke up to coffee. That's why he was brimming at the sight of the underground tastemaker, Head. It meant that Head had found someone to help him get at a rival.

Fooley Wayne tapped the chest of Head's sweater and motioned for him to follow him. But upon seeing that Head wanted to snatch his wrist off his frame, he tried to smooth things out. Head stood as tall as an ape and was cloaked in two hundred sixty pounds of solid girth. The type of girth that made people feign nice to him all his life. Or, in a street sense—tread lightly. This was exactly how Head preferred it. And seeing that Fooley Wayne got the memo, he brushed it off and followed him towards the kitchen, listening as he teased that if the girls kept this up, he would sic him on them.

"Best believe I gotta place for 'em," Head said, referring to the pretentious dice house where he offered sex. "They can bring they spoiled rich asses over to The Shack and get in where they fit in."

Fooley Wayne posted up against the shiny marble kitchen island. "Speaking of The Shack, tell them trap niggas I ain't running with my winnings. I shoot dice. That's what I do. I just got a crazy ass schedule. Matter of fact, next time my shit clears up, I'ma bring some of my celebrity friends through and we gon' make this trip more legendary than the first." He continued when he saw a smile on Head's face. "I'm talkin' a private school tuition on the floor type shit." Fooley Wayne was a master at tapping into the likes of others. After he finished schmoozing, he got right down to business. "Head, I appreciate you coming through. This shit with C.T. Shiesty is gettin' out of hand. He really holding his nuts on a nigga. Man, look at what this hoe ass nigga done did."

Head blocked Fooley Wayne from pulling out his phone as if he was trying to hand him a gun in front of the police. "Hold on," he protested, looking around the room at all the eyes and ears. It wasn't like they were talking about pizza. "You tryna do this right here?"

Nonchalantly glancing towards the glass booth in the far corner, Fooley Wayne suggested, "I mean, would you feel more comfortable in the studio?" Head sighed and looked off as if to collect himself. He was usually a quiet person but right now that quiet was speaking volumes for him. Fooley Wayne followed his drift. "Oh, you want privacy, I get it. That's all you had to say. Just gimme a second to clear this bitch out." Immediately, Fooley Wayne took off towards the clout-chasing women, a few friends from his old neighborhood, and a couple people he didn't even know. "Alright, party's over." His words sobered everyone as if he'd cut the music. "Time to go." He gestured for everybody to get up, but a pretty girl took offense.

"Time to go?" She snaked her neck.

"Yeah, love." He plucked the blunt from her pink tips. "Time to go. An emergency came up. We gon' have to do this another time." When she stood and he saw that ass, he secretly wished she could stay. But some of the guys he was more familiar with weren't moving fast enough. "Yeah, dawg. That mean y'all too." They weren't tripping. They showed him love before they bounced.

A lone stranger grabbed a bottle of Rémy as he was leaving.

"You won't be needing this. Iight, pimpin'. Fuck with you." Fooley Wayne closed the door and turned back towards Head. "Now where were we?" The feel of his phone made him answer his own question. "Oh, yeah. This hoe ass nigga, C.T. Shiesty."

Fooley Wayne placed the drugs down on a rare table like it was one at a cheap motel, then passed Head his phone to view a video. He was growing animated. He mentioned how previously he just wanted somebody to rough his opp up. But now he was thirsty to see the Charlotte native, C.T. Shiesty's blood.

"Man, the nigga brought my kid up. Can you believe this shit? Out of all the things in the world, the nigga brought up my son." He watched the video with Head for a minute before he revealed more layers. "Now, he out here in the D doing a show tonight. Shooting slugs about, he can go anywhere he want and a nigga ain't gon' do shit. He think shit sweet," His agitation spread throughout his body. "But I'm tryna send a different message by the end of the night."

Fooley Wayne was hotter than a dope boy that just got robbed, and understandably so. A few months ago, C.T. Shiesty started dry plexin' with him during a New York radio interview, saying that he didn't think that Fooley Wayne was as street as everyone thought. This instigated everything. And after a scuffle between their squads at a Miami party, the verbal blows gradually became more contentious.

"I agree," Head said. "A message gotta be sent. Ain't no nigga coming through the D on that fuck shit. And I got just the person to do it." Head found optimism in Fooley Wayne's eyes. "Are you familiar with my nigga 200?"

"Hold up. Wait. You talkin' *thee* 200? 200 out of Highland Hills? Mr. Rob-A-Plug himself?" he asked. "Hell yeah, I know who 200 is. If a nigga got a bag and wanna keep it, they *bedda* know."

"Well, he knows who you are too. And after I explained the situation, he said that he would consider offering his expertise. But—" his short pause indicated that there was a catch. "He wasn't too thrilled about the twenty-five K you was talkin'. Something about gettin' at a famous person. But how about I just link y'all up so y'all can sort that shit out yaselves?"

Fooley Wayne could already see the headline his new hitta would create. He extended his hand. "That's a bet. How soon can you get him to come through?"

***

Queen felt a hint of exhilaration as she was pinned against the front door, looking down as 200 devoured her. She could feel the knocks reverberating from the other side through her back, and it heightened her pleasure as well as the pulsing of her heart.

"Gi-give him a minute," Queen did her best to muffle her sensual sounds, but she couldn't hold out any longer. "Ooh... fuck!" Her eyes bucked in embarrassment then her voice lowered, "See what you did?"

"What?" 200 asked.

"Now your cousin gon' be looking at me like I'm some type of thot."

"Who cares what he think?" 200 dove back in.

"I do."

200 brushed that off before planting more pleasurable kisses. "'Can't nobody make you something you not. Didn't yo mama name you Queen?"

"Yeah," she panted, biting down on her lip and helplessly giving in. "But you know I got a vendor to go meet. And I thought your meeting with your cousin was important."

200 kissed her southern lips as if they were a reconciling couple. "You're important to me." Then he slid two fingers inside her and worked his magic until she was sounding more angelic than Jhene Aiko. This was the type of tongue action that would leave a girl's head gone, and he didn't let up until she screamed and shouted from an orgasm. But he wasn't done with little Miss Wet-Wet—not even in the least bit. She was taking 200's course on how to treat her man right now. And he was using sex as a tool to teach it.

200 stepped out of his clothes then freed her right ankle from her pants. He ignored her reminders that his cousin was outside and that he was gonna make her late. Instead, he flipped that petite bubble towards him and thrusted that dick inside.

"Unt-uh! What you doing? You gotta take it easy!" Queen braced herself on the door.

200 kept busting her up. "I ain't taking shit easy. I'm mad at you right now."

68

"About what? What I do?" she pouted.

"It ain't what you did, it's more like what you didn't do." 200 grabbed her professionally dyed hair and pulled her head just enough to speak in her ear. "From now on I don't want you being uncomfortable talking to me about anything. We in this. And we don't keep secrets from each other." He thrusted harder. "Am I clear?" He was referring to when he walked in their bedroom and saw Queen on the phone engaged in a heated and emotional argument with her father, something the natural beauty half-heartedly downplayed. But 200 knew that there was more to it.

Nevertheless, he should've been the last person bringing up secrets. Poor Queen didn't know that 200 was set to be in court next Thursday, or that he was racing to meet PG's deadline. Or the fact that he may be living on borrowed time. But she felt it in every stroke. Because he always hit the pussy like it would be their last time.

"Okay. Okay!"

"Okay, what?" 200 kept her from running.

"Okay, we're clear. I won't keep no secrets from you."

"And what else?"

"Oh shit, I forgot. I don't know. I'm 'bout to... cum."

The left side of Queen's face found the door like a pillow while 200 slid in and out of her stomach, driving her to the most intense orgasm she ever had. She was loud enough for 200's guest to hear her from his car. And it had 200 feeling like he was that guy. He looked down at the way she was coating him to admire his handiwork. And it had his dick building up like a bag of microwave popcorn.

Minutes later, he was popping his seeds deep inside her. A trip into outer space couldn't have felt better.

"You my baby." 200 kissed her neck. "You my mufuckin' baby." He turned her so he could look in her alluring eyes, then kissed her with a fervor that reached her heart. Losing herself, she started to kiss him back. But then thinking about her meeting, she said, "Damn," and pushed him away. "Boy, I'm already running late. And now I gotta redo my hair."

200 caught her before she made any real leeway towards the bathroom. "Queen," he called.

"What?"

"I love you."

This made her steps halt. She sashayed back toward him with a glowing smirk on her face. She clasped her hands around his neck, and softly said, "I love you too." She gave him a sweet peck then hurried to freshen up. 200's eyes fell to the crack of her ass. It made him want to run her down like a preying animal. This girl had definitely become his.

***

Back in the living room, after 200 had hit his grill, Monte dried a blunt then offered it to 200 to do the honors. 200 flicked the lighter with no hesitation. He sat forward to get more comfortable then became apologetic about having him wait outside in the car. "Don't trip. If anybody understands, I do," Monte assured. After he hit the blunt, he looked around and added, "Man, this is a nice ass crib."

200 had started telling him how his baby came from a good family and had started her own company just as she entered the room. She shined with the glow of love in her eyes as she slid behind 200 and gave him a hug and quick smooch.

"Bye, babe," Queen said, then smiled with friendliness and waved goodbye to Monte. 200 tried to call out to her before she left. "Hey, I prolly won't be in till late. But good luck with your vendor."

Monte innocently shook his head in admiration as she flew out the door. "Damn, brains *and* booty. Girls like that travel in packs. Now where the cousins at?" He tugged the stubble on his chin.

200 laughed. "You crazy!"

"Nah, what's crazy is you bagged this fine ass chick with all this money. And you sitting here playing all cool like you Denzel. Cuz, you bedda than me. I'd be tryna get her ass pregnant."

Seeing that Monte was so excited, 200 rehashed how their first date was this wild and crazy trip to Vegas. "Yeah, I just asked her on the spot if she wanted to go. And we pretty much been on some best friends shit ever since."

"That's the bestie, huh?"

"Yeah, no doubt. Especially now. I been going through it, and she been right there to lift me up." 200 saw that his revelation had caused a silence in the room. Monte was aware of Renee's murder, but he didn't know the half of why it happened and the dangers facing him and Jaylen. "Look, I gotta come clean about something." This was the reason why 200 had called him over.

Monte flipped one of his plaits out of his face. "Okay, alright. Give it to me."

"Well, I told you over at Doonie's how the Twinz crossed me out on that lick. But what I didn't tell you is how I'm at war with the people of the family we robbed. They're called The Golliday Boyz, but it's mainly this dopeboy named PG, with deep connections. These niggas is threatening to kill Jaylen if they don't get their bread. And they the ones..." he started, before clenching his jaw, "...they the ones who killed my Dukes."

It was impossible not to feel the anger and hurt in 200's heart. It was possible easier to trek through Alaska and not get cold.

"Whoa... that's some heavy shit. And I hate to see you over there going through it. But why you just didn't take me up on my offer? I told you I'm ridin'."

"Well, for starters, I was embarrassed."

"Embarrassed?" Monte scoffed.

"Yeah. Everybody looks at me like I'm bulletproof. And here I am, showing chinks in my armor."

200's statement left Monte flabbergasted.

"My dude, everybody look at you like you bulletproof, 'cause you *really* like that. You don't bar none. That's why when the streets think of Dallas, they think of you," he reminded. "And if you fight through this for lil' bro like only you can, the name 200 will forever ring bells."

"Well, that's something you ain't gotta worry 'bout, cause hanging Jaylen out to dry ain't even an option. I'ma make sure my brother is safe. And when it's all said and done, I'ma find a way to get at PG." 200 went on to tell him how serious The Golliday Boyz were, how much information they had on him, and why he had to tread lightly. He explained how they already retrieved half their loot. "But right now I'm having problems coming up with a substantial amount of money."

"Cuz, if it's money you need, then why not just come back up top with me and hit this lick on my boss? I'm telling you," Monte stressed, "this the one that's gon' put you over the top."

200 was adamant. "Nah, Cuz, I can't be making no detours to the 'Lou. I got ten days to get this money to him. And I gotta hurry up before it's too late."

"Alright," Monte conceded, "you drive, and I'll ride shot. We gotta get this money for lil' Cuz. Just point me towards the target and I'll be ready to shoot."

200 showed his appreciation with a strong handshake. "Bet. In that case, lemme tell you about this next move then. Are you familiar with the rapper Fooley Wayne?"

"Hell, yeah. That nigga plex'd up with ol' boy C.T. Shiesty. I was just on the Gram out in the car, looking at their beef."

A sinister smile covered 200's face. "Well, that's our next move. Fooley Wayne wants us to get at that nigga C. T. Shiesty for him."

Chapter 11

200 and Monte stood on the gold-trimmed elevator and had just pressed the floor for Fooley Wayne's studio when someone approached to enter. The white guy, whose glasses spelled he belonged in the Ivy League, saw the elevator's occupants and decided to wait for the next one. Smart man. Maybe he knew they had it on their minds. Energy could speak volumes and right now, theirs were speaking trouble.

After the elevator closed, sealing off the noises of the lobby, 200 looked over at Monte and asked, "You ready?"

Monte's dark skin showed assurance. "Ready as I'll ever be. Whateva kinda message the nigga want sent, if it benefits the fam, I'm all for it."

200 felt a measure of solace, seeing that Monte was stomp down. It had been awhile since he had someone formidable on the team and he was convinced that Monte was twice as deadly and loyal.

A pleasant *ting* announced that they had arrived on the twelfth floor. 200 was the first to move, while Monte quickly followed suit, brushing lint from his designer clothes as he stepped down the art-filled corridor. 200 had told him to dress like they were about to hit a venue. Not that he was trying to blend in. Here, a good percentage of the residents looked like them. 200 just didn't want to be seen here wearing the same clothes that they were gon' step in later. He was still as meticulous as ever, which was probably why he'd been able to get away with such big dirt for so long.

Speaking so only they could hear, they walked a short distance until they stood in front of Fooley Wayne's studio. 200 took a deep breath then knocked on the door. A few seconds later, a dude just as large as an NFL lineman filled the doorway.

"200, right?" asked the brown-skinned bouncer. "Fooley's expecting you. Come on," he waved. "Step inside."

200 enjoyed the decadent scenery but did his best not to act struck. He had one thing, and one thing only, on his mind—business.

Spotting a shirtless Fooley Wayne inside the glass booth, 200 made a beeline for the studio's entrance. He had only been inside the spacious residence for five seconds.

"Nah… nah… nah… nah… nah! Don't go in there, he recording right now."

200 kept walking.

"Nigga, is you deaf?" the bouncer barked. "I said he's in there recording!"

The bouncer's words hit 200 like a slur had been hurled in his direction. He turned on his heels and stormed towards the bouncer, like he was the one that was six-seven and three hundred pounds.

"Yo," 200 stepped to him. "If you wanna keep them lips on yo' face, I suggest you start acting like you know who the fuck you talking to." Whatever 200 was clutching inside his jacket wasn't nearly as threatening as the look on his face. "Now get yo' ass over there and tell him we out here."

200 didn't even watch to see if he followed his order. He walked right over to the plush sitting area with Monte flanking him and sat back on the couch as if he was at home. The subtle bounce caused the woman's perfume next to him to rise. He glanced over and gave her a neutral nod, as if to say, *"what's up."* He was oblivious to the fact that the dime piece he'd just spoken to, who was batting her flowing lashes at him, was the newest R&B singer signed to Quality Control. She dug the respect he commanded, his rugged appearance, and that special something that said he was in control. If she was in the business of pursuing niggas, then she would definitely get at him.

"You got a light?" she asked, once she finished rolling a blunt. She deliberately ignored the fact that she had one in her pocket.

200 patted the breast pocket of his black Moncler jacket. It seemed the more he looked at her, the more attraction he found. Suddenly, he was the perfect gentleman, holding the light to her lips. But before she could pass the blunt to him, an animated Fooley Wayne appeared from the studio, holding his hands in the air.

"Well, if it isn't the man 200 himself. What up, cousin?" The way Fooley Wayne spoke to him, it was as if they had known each other for years.

200 came to the middle of the room where Fooley Wayne stood. "According to the city, *you* what's up." He lowered his voice. "Tell me what I gotta do to keep it that way."

Fooley Wayne patted him on the shoulder and looked around. It was obvious he was doped up or something. "Follow me." Unlike earlier when it was essentially a party, there were only three other people there besides them. He'd already told the engineer that he would need some privacy. So, they had the control room to the studio all to themselves. Fooley Wayne went to the ledge of the control panel and grabbed one of an assortment of pills.

"My bad," Fooley Wayne apologized for the detour. "This beef with C.T. Shiesty got me all the way discombobulated," he admitted. "I feel like if I don't take something to slow me down, I'ma jump out on the nigga myself." After the three shared a laugh, Fooley Wayne asked, "Did Head lace you up?"

200 deliberated on the question before he answered. "Yup, he filled me in. And on his word that you were serious, I went right to work. I learned that C.T. arrived here at noon, and he's staying at the Omni. They prearranged to have a rented black 'Massi there for him, and it's been in the same spot all day. Hmm, what else? He's scheduled to hit the stage tonight at eleven, but he's likely to arrive at nine. And all that shit about coming through the 'D' one-deep was some bullshit. He brought at least one lil' dark-skinned nigga with him."

"Damn," Fooley Wayne was dumbfounded, "you learned all that shit since Head left?"

"I learned everything except for what kind of message you want sent. What exactly do you want done?" 200 asked, leaving murder on the menu.

"Actually, I just want his jewels. I want the nigga to see that he can be touched. I want to humiliate him. But you ain't gotta kill 'em. Even though he brought up my son, I don't want that shit falling back on me."

This was a relief to 200, but his face didn't show it. Murdering a celebrity would surely bring down police heat. He didn't have room for anything to interrupt his mission.

"So, you don't want me to kill him, and you want his jewels," 200 repeated. "Fine. I can do that. But it's gonna run ya fifty K."

"Fifty... ohh," Fooley Wayne said as if it hurt.

"Yeah, fifty's the ticket. And that's just to keep me and my shooter from shooting." 200 rested against the sound board. "That nigga really had me in my feelings the way he was coming at you. Nigga, this my city. C.T. is Dallas's new mayor. A real killa can go anywhere he wants. But you see now, it's deeper than some rap shit. You represent us, and niggas gon' know that them boys in the 'D' ain't playing no games."

Seeing Fooley Wayne in thought, 200 tried to drive home his point. "Besides, you want shit done right. Your career is going too good to have it derailed by some street punk that might panic when it could cost you most. You my brutha," he started, "you need professionals."

"But fifty K, my nigga?"

"Fifty K." 200 stood his ground. "And it's gon' need to hit my hands before I leave."

There seemed to be some apprehension on Fooley Wayne's part.

***

"You muthafuckin' right I followed you," a woman could be heard yelling. "Why is my man about to walk inside the club with another bitch!"

Their toxic argument flowed twenty yards away to a dark stolen Lexus, making 200 shrink in the driver's seat in discomfort. Currently, it was 9:03. C.T. and Shiest was due to arrive at Prime Bar's lush complex at any minute. But here these mufuckas were, blowing up the spot.

"Ooh," Tasha gasped, covering her mouth. "No, she didn't." The confronting girl had reached and snatched a blue track out the head of her man's creeper. As a group of muscle-bound men rushed the lot to intervene, another security guard ran his flashlight inside the interior of the Lexus. It felt like they'd been caught trying to enter a building. If they were guilty of one thing, it was looking the part. When most patrons hit the club's lot, they usually fell right in. So, it stood out that they were still sitting inside the car. His flashlight lingered on their wide eyes a little longer before he went about his way.

Monte seemed to feel the tension more than anyone. "Am I tripping? Or is there a lot going on out here?"

"Nah, you ain't tripping. They is," 200 answered. "I wish they would hurry up and get this shit under control, before this nigga pull up."

Five minutes later, 200's wish was granted. Well, mostly. The ratchet couple had left, but one of the security guards still lingered, paying an unwanted amount of attention to their car.

"His bitch ass need to fall in the club." 200 grew testy. "We don't need no added eyewitnesses or super cops trying to save the day." This time 200's wish was taking longer to come to fruition, too long. He found himself playing with the turtleneck sleeve of his Under Armor shirt when the black 'Massi they'd been waiting for hit the lot. His words made a nervous excitement contagious inside the car. "That might be him over there, pulling in the owner's spot."

They began to watch the car like a hawk. 200's eyes cut back and forth between him and the guard. Thoughts raced inside his mind as action continued to culminate. *Will this nigga just leave?*

C.T. Shiesty parked the car and killed the lights, and his partner emerged from the vehicle.

Wrong place, wrong time, thought 200. *I wonder if the club security guard is armed.*

C.T. Shiesty's portly figure and distinct bald head exited the car.

"That's him." 200 concealed his identity with the turtleneck.

"Fuck it, let's go!" Monte concealed his identity as well as he spilled out of the car. The only thing identifiable was the glistening chrome of his gun. They stalked forward as quietly as two panthers, but probably more dangerous. Monte made that known when he announced their arrival by filling C.T.'s potna with a slug.

B'ough!

Now the menacing barrels were pointed at C.T. "Look, if you don't want these next slugs going in you, I suggest you get yo' ass on the ground," 200 warned. C.T.'s expression hinted that he wanted to buck. "Or would you prefer I do it for you?" 200 threatened.

Seconds were precious, and there was no telling if the other guard ran in the club to get help. Reluctantly, C.T. Shiesty got down on his knees with his hands in the air. Before he found some courage, 200 made himself clear. "Run the muthafuckin' jewels." 200 looked towards the door. "All of them." He came off close to a hundred fifty thousand dollars in jewelry, including a new sparkling diamond choker. When the jewels hit 200's hands, it was like C.T. Shiesty had passed him a baton.

He took off running, while Monte backpedaled towards the car, ready to shoot. His trigger finger was itchy, like he contracted some type of disease. *A nigga bet not play.*

***

After leaving the whip with Tasha to ditch, and changing back into more appropriate clothes, 200's Tahoe silhouetted outside of the studio an hour later. Future's music was deadened when he killed the engine. But Monte's laughter quickly filled that void.

"What?" 200 asked, softening to his expression.

"Man, you gotta see this. Look," Monte held out his phone, "check this out."

200 squinted his beady eyes at the image on YouTube. It was captioned "Slow Day" and it featured none other than the guy they were here to see, Fooley Wayne. Pressing play, the glowing screen transported him inside the studio. The house producer had hit a button that lightly ran Dej Loaf's "Try Me," while Fooley Wayne entertained himself counting bands. From 200's trained eye, it appeared to be eighty racks. He became intrigued when Fooley Wayne started to rock to the beat. Seconds later, he began to play around on the track.

"Get at me?" Fooley Wayne laughed. "Nigga, I'll put two in something/then swerve off ·in some big wheels like I'm two or something. I got street ties/ catch me mobbin', might see *Two* or something…"

"You hear that shit?" Monte slapped 200's arm. "That nigga just dropped your name!" He was all excited and giddy, but he urged him to keep viewing.

Suddenly, the hyped producer stood and told Fooley Wayne that he was goin' in too hard, making Fooley Wayne end his impromptu session with a laugh. Then the music lowered and the person behind the camera asked him a question.

"You hear about that shit that happened with C.T. Shiesty?"

"Nah. What happened?"

"His people got shot, and he got robbed right outside of Prime Bar before his show."

"No shit?" Fooley Wayne asked.

"Word," the recorder responded.

"Damn that's fucked up. You know we had our differences, but I don't wish that shit on nobody," he said solemnly. For a moment, Fooley Wayne seemed genuine and even his expression showed it. But when he spoke again, his tone said it was all a ruse. "Welp, let me get back to counting this bread."

The screen went black, and Monte turned up. His phone stayed in his hand. This was really his type of shit. "Man, that nigga Fooley Wayne a fool. That nigga too turnt. He didn't even wait for C.T.'s people to get patched up good before he hopped on the web and sent out subliminals."

For as hard as Monte was smiling, 200's face was stone. "Yo, when did he make this?"

Monte checked. "It was posted ten minutes ago."

"C'mon. Let's head inside." 200 stepped out the truck but Monte seemed confused.

"Aren't you gon' grab the jewelry?"

"Mmm… I guess." 200 doubled back. He seemed hesitant to bring the jewelry. Something wasn't right. As they walked under the lobby's opulent fixtures then entered the elevator, 200 began to whisper where only Monte could hear. Funny, because there wasn't anybody else in the car.

200 continued this as they exited, walking a hair slower towards Fooley Wayne's studio. By the time they approached it, Monte shared 200's stone face. 200 knocked on the door and the bouncer he'd charged up was still there. All seemed well, and he welcomed them inside with a nod. In the instant it took to adjust to the room's cool temperature, 200 processed who was there. The bouncer they'd passed, the producer by the wet bar. *And... oh, there goes Fooley Wayne.*

"Muthafuckin', 200. Job well done." Fooley Wayne smiled and clapped with a gallantry reserved for someone winning an award. He moved towards the center of the room as 200 did the same.

"See, I told you," 200 started, sharing a celebratory smile. "You was all hesitant to pay me before the job. But I told you that you needed professionals, and this is what professionals do." He pulled a small, neutral-colored sack from his coat. He slowly opened it, and a cache of quality jewels began to gleam. Everyone looked on in awe at the white bluish stones, and Fooley Wayne was one of the first to grab one of the pieces. His squad followed suit.

As they stood in the middle of the chic room, captivated by the jewels, 200 and Monte peered on from over their shoulders. The men with the jewels were laughing and cappin', but there was a wild excitement racing through the goons. Monte broke their sneaky silence by whacking the bouncer in the back of his bald head with the tool, spurting blood on Fooley Wayne's expensive white V-neck. From there, it seemed like a melee ensued, spawned by loud curses of panic, shoes screeching, and the thud of the bouncer's unconscious body hitting the floor. But 200 quieted it all when he jacked a live round in his pistol's chamber. He aimed the gaping barrel at the blue streaked dread dangling over Fooley Wayne's face.

"Yo, where that money you posted on the Gram?"

"Money? What money?" Seeing 200 tighten his grip, his hands shot up. "What you talking 'bout, fam? I already paid you."

"I see this nigga right here having trouble understanding what you mean." Monte stepped over the bouncer. "Maybe when he hear these slugs he'll know that we serious." Mouth tightening, Monte mashed the trigger, hoping to hear his favorite sound, but all he heard was a light click.

"Fam, did you take the safety off?" 200 asked.

Monte looked at the slide. "Oh." Shaking his blunder, he quickly aimed the pistol at the bouncer's vulnerable body and was about to squeeze, before Fooley Wayne's hurried insistence halted him.

"Hold up! Hold up!" he pleaded with his hands. "Please don't shoot."

"Hold up for what, nigga?" 200's face screwed. "I told you we wanted the loot. You acting all dumb. So, ain't shit else to talk about."

"Alright… look, nah, don't shoot! Just look. The money is in the sound room. You'll see it in a Dior bag on the board." Unbeknownst to the goons, the bouncer was actually Fooley Wayne's older brother.

Monte made the other two men get down on the floor next to the bouncer. "Go 'head and grab that, too. I got this shit out here." And that wasn't cap. Monte was really pump faking when he aimed the pistol at the bouncer. If he wanted to, he could've killed them as easily as killing some roaches. He methodically retrieved the jewels that they heisted from C.T. Shiesty, as well as an icy bracelet off of Fooley Wayne, along with everything else they had of value. 200 walked back in with the bag just as he was tucking it.

"Was it in there?" Monte asked.

"Yeah, the bands and a lil FN."

"That's what's up. I got the jewels, plus a piece off of Fooley Wayne too."

"That's good. If this nigga think about going to the police, we can sell this to C.T. so he could do a lil' cappin."

"I got an even better idea." Monte pulled out his phone and started recording. After capturing what he thought was sufficient footage, he warned Fooley Wayne. "Yeah, play with your career if you want to. But I'm sure you'll lose a lot of fans if they see their favorite gangsta hulled out like this."

As they cautiously moved towards the door, 200 added, "Yeah, that name drop was banging too. Make sure you go ahead and finish that track."

Chapter 12

Sabrina plopped down on a sky-blue ottoman, then took a deep breath. Lil Jason was napping. She had finished her online studies for the day. Instead of serving brunch, she *became* it for her bae, PG, who had just left. Now, it was time to watch somebody unwind in their pretentious surroundings and this wasn't just any somebody, this was hands down the baddest baddie reppin' the D— *me*, she affirmed.

Grabbing the smart remote, Sabrina aimed it at the bedroom's 5G television, then hit the power button with a little pizzazz. A Lakers game, *no*. Whitney Houston's documentary, *I've seen that.*

Oh, this looks like something good. She left the channel on *Lifetime*. Though, if the network wanted drama, they'd base a show around her. Because her relationship had all the telltale signs of one of the toxic ones.

Currently, Sabrina sat in her impressive Plano home, which PG brokered from one of Slick's political contacts. She was rockin' an expensive black chiffon robe that was purchased on a PG sponsored spree. She still had the taste of PG's flavored lip balm on everything from her small baby bump to her clit from their recent tryst. But the first thing she thought about when PG left was 200, the man she swore she would leave alone.

They say love makes you do some crazy things, and Sabrina was unconsciously doing just that. It was less than two months ago when she told her older man, PG, that the police wanted to question 200 for his siblings' murders. Their relationship had rapidly grown serious, and she wanted to give PG closure. Or maybe she hated 200 more than she cared to admit. He did play games with her heart and had squandered the remainder of the money she'd gotten after her grandmother's death. But it was like hearing 200's emotional voicemail sprouted seeds that he once planted in her heart. Damn the fact that 200 didn't know that she was with PG. Damn the dangerous war that was taking place behind her naïve little back. 200 had brought back sentiments only he could bring to her heart. This left her fighting an insurmountable desire to call him back.

Okay this is getting good. Sabrina curbed the thought and tried to dive into the show. But it didn't take long before 200 was back on her mind. She smirked as she mused about the days when he was all she saw. Before she realized it, her pink Samsung was in her hand. She took a breath to relax, then told herself, *this is strictly for closure.* When in the back of her mind, she was longing for that old thing. She began to text.

//: Hey 2. Its bn so long since we talked I dnt even know where to start. I guess by sayn sorry about what happen to your mother. I know that ur hurtn ... I wish

Before Sabrina could text that she wished she could be there for him, a shadow blocked all the light in the room like an eclipse. She almost broke her neck trying to see what it was.

"PG...bae, I-I didn't even hear you come in." She dropped the phone.

"Oh, I had to slide back to grab my charger. But it didn't hurt to see you in here looking all good." PG's words slowed the rapid pacing of her heart, even though he was frowning more and smiling less. "C'mere," he said, inching towards the crane of her neck. His sexy lips found that spot he knew drove her wild.

"Baby," she whined when his strong hand opened her robe and caressed her breast. PG's sensual assault was relentless. She knew where this would lead. "Just lemme go freshen up real quick." She stood, smiling.

Gripping her succulent ass, PG planted a few more kisses. "Go 'head and hurry up, you got me wanting that shit right now." PG followed the clap of her ass as she scurried into the bathroom. When he heard the water come on, his eyes darted to the phone on the ottoman. Remembering her suspicious behavior, he picked it up. Now he was feeling the old adage, *don't go prying for what you don't want to see.* "That's crazy, she fuckin' with this nigga again." He wouldn't confront her about it. But this was something his callous mind wouldn't forget.

Chapter 13

200 hopped out of the Tahoe in front of Queen's spot, then closed the door so hard that mired ice fell from under the fender. It seemed he was fucked up about something when he really was tired. He had been running the streets for the past two days with no sleep and didn't have the wherewithal to stop the door from slamming like a wild heathen did it. Nature seemed to be begging to take its course. Looking on the side of the Tahoe, his tatted reflection appeared, wearing a tan winter coat and clutching a bag that wasn't nearly as big as the ones under his eyes. But his efforts weren't in vain. He did juice this Philly nigga with a brick of Recon that he believed was dope, then robbed a heavy hitta in his car who was too naïve to look up from counting his cash. But the majority of his time was spent casing out an illegal game room.

In Texas, casino gambling was prohibited. So, people flocked to the illegal game rooms to support their vice. 200 found this one in a shady shopping center not far from 35th and Beckley. It had been on his radar since he ran with the Twinz. If he could make this pop, he would be that much closer to squaring his debt with PG.

He walked inside the newly built home and relaxed at the sight of the familiar chic furnishings. The home was quiet, in a peaceful way, and he couldn't wait to crash out for a few hours of sleep. After he secured his money and shed his coat, he went upstairs in search of Queen. The closer he got to the top, the more he heard the shower going. Then seeing steam flowing from under the bathroom door, he calmly announced himself, "Baby?" Opening the door, he started to announce himself again, then he heard her painful sobs and immediately softened up.

He pulled the foggy glass door open, and Queen was standing under the water with her hands covering her face.

He didn't ask her what was wrong. He simply guided her out of the shower and held her in his comforting arms. He showered her with self-assuring kisses as he ushered her back to their bedroom.

Then 200 fell back onto the bed with her without even bothering to take off his clothes. He just wanted to let her know he was there for her. Nothing else mattered now. He pulled the maroon comforter over her nakedness as she lay atop his chest. He absorbed the unrestrained heaves leaving her body as if they had left his own. Then after pushing a strand of hair behind her ear, he kissed one of her tears away and asked, "What's wrong?"

It took Queen a second to discipline her heaves. "Nothing, Two. Nothing."

"Awl, here we go with this again. I know we ain't back on that. I told you I wanted you to be comfortable talking to me about anything. Now tell me, what's going on?"

Queen finally raised her head and looked at him. Even though her eyes were tear-stained, he could still see the angel in her. And even more so, he saw the trust in them. Her adorable lips parted. "You remember how I was on the phone arguing with my father?"

"Yeah."

"Well, he called again and this time, things got even worse."

200 didn't understand how she could argue with a man as generous as her father. He knew that he and her stepmom spoiled her rotten. But he just stayed quiet and listened.

"You're so easy to read. You see all the material possessions and think everything's just peaches and cream. But my family is a wreck. An absolute wreck! My God..." Queen paused, pinching the bridge of her nose at the thought. "Okay, I'ma tell you why we were arguing, but don't start judging me."

200 balked. "Nah, I ain't with that shit. I don't want you judging *me*, so why would I do that to you?"

"Well, if you remember, I told you that my mother died of natural causes, because growing up that's what I was taught. But over the years, my father either lost track of his lie or became complacent. Because now whenever I ask how she died, the answer always changes. But I think he's the one who did it. Nah, I *know* he did it! That's what my instincts are telling me. And my instincts are rarely wrong."

"Your father though?"

"Yes, my father, Jason. They stayed arguing like cats and dogs. Mainly over this murder he claimed she was hanging over his head. I don't remember what it was, per se. I was seven years old, but he always threatened that he would kill her if she ever told anyone. I remember *that*. That much, I do remember," Queen was adamant. "Then one day, my dad picked me up early from school. And I was rushed to the hospital where my ill mother..." she air quoted, "...suddenly passed."

"Is that your mother right there?" 200 asked about the gorgeous fair-skinned lady in the antique frame by the bed.

"That's both of my parents." She began to grow enamored with the picture of her mom. "He did it. I know he did. Nobody else could have done it but him."

200 squeezed her with all he had as they laid back together.

"It's gone be alright, ma. It's gone be alright." He was hoping that would go for both of their situations.

Chapter 14

Tasha sat at a slot machine inside Shelly's game room, disguised in a black wig and shades that hid her drip and made her look like an average hood hoe. But she wasn't alone. It was definitely some hoes in this house, doing everything from sneaking into private rooms to smoking bo's in plain sight. Shelly's was considered a hole in the wall. But people still flocked to the underground staple because they had the best paying slots. It was 2:00 am and the place was crackin'. Tasha's slot machine kept going nuts like a cash register, but neither the machine nor her mission was strong enough to break her concentration from all that smoke.

Her chocolate face scrunched as she looked over at Monte. "All this ice or whateva they smoking is making my head hurt. We need to hurry up and get this done so we can leave."

Monte, who was disguised in a ballcap and a covid mask, countered with no sympathy, "You a big girl. You can handle it."

This made Tasha's neck roll like Cardi B in the flesh. "Oh, I can handle a lot of things—you being one of them. But this funny smelling shit is too much. And it's getting on my nerves." Taking heed to what he was really saying, Tasha quit pouting and put her head back in the game. She knew the six-figure payday they had at stake and how important this was to 200. Glancing at her tatted wrist, she noticed 200 had been gone for ten minutes to case the place, one final round. In reaction, her heartbeat sped like a roller coaster. She knew it was about to go down.

"You see that white guy over there with the blonde ponytail, the big one?" Tasha whispered to Monte. "Don't look now. But it seems he's been keeping his eyes on us. Then you got these chinks walking the floor, eyeing everybody like they suspect. Everybody knows they kick people out at their own discretion. I'm just hoping we won't stand out." Any Chinese people here were presumed to be a part of this underground establishment, putting them on the wrong side of this six-figure play.

As Tasha listened to Monte soothe her worries, a chubby chink with thick auburn hair headed their way. "Oh, shit. Here one comes. Hug me, just to play it off." The hugging part she added on her own. She low-key dug that Monte was cute, cutthroat, and didn't give a fuck, a recipe for getting her pussy wet. Pulling back, she wiped a smudge of lip gloss she accidentally left on his cheek. She was really just having fun being all up on him.

"You sure we don't need to do that again—you know… to play it off?" Monte flirted.

"Maybe later." She led him on. Having that stripper's pedigree, Tasha looked at sex like a nigga. But she was still reserved enough to know that if anybody was getting this pussy, it was 200. Just as she was growing antsy about his

91

whereabouts, he appeared at her side, camouflaged like a trail riding country boy.

"Y'all need to get on your toes," 200 spoke low and clipped, but with enough intensity to stoke a fire. "I found what I believe to be their count room. And from the looks, it's only three Chinks left. Three of them… three of us," he professed when he heard a small commotion. A small commotion swelled into a large commotion and before you knew it, all hell broke loose.

"Get down on the ground! Police!" several men yelled, coming out of their disguises and showing their badges and lettered vests.

200 eyed the team thinking, *what the fuck,* before quickly rebounding and urging, "C'mon." He led them through the low-lit area towards one of the mapped-out exits. People were damn near trampling over each other trying to get somewhere. Most were harboring small amounts of drugs, but 200 and Monte were wanted for serious crimes.

"Get down on the ground … Now!" A lone white officer blocked their path. They all tried to barrel past him, but when he grabbed Monte's shoulder, shit got real. Monte didn't hesitate. By the time the officer spun him around, he was already firing at everything that's vital.

Boom! Boom! Boom! Boom! Boom!

Instead of freezing like a dog in the middle of the street, 200 sent shots to the ceiling to create more chaos. People got low. As they dipped out of the line of fire, they darted down the wood paneled hallway, closing in on their rehearsed exit. 200 saw the men's bathroom door swinging back and forth, then figured Tasha had already pushed her way through. They followed her trail like a dog chasing a scent, past the stalls, out the window, and into the crisp cold of the night.

Thirty Minutes Later

200 paced around the living room at the Baby Ritz, shaking his head. "Damn, that was it right there. We were this close to being able to cover PG's money. Now we done fucked around and shot a bunch of cops."

It grew silent as Tasha and Monte both sat on the couch, quiet as church mice, rehashing in their own heads how things could have played out. They all knew this was the big chance. But what were they to do, the laws had other plans.

"Look, you and I both know that it's 'bout to get hotter than fish grease around this mufucka," Monte reasoned. "We didn't make the score and what's done is done. But what you need to do is, come back to the 'Lou with me like I said, and take care of this nigga Lil Ronnie. I don't know why you ain't been did the shit. The bread we chasing ain't shit in comparison to what he holding."

"And what type of bread is that again?" 200 asked, pinching his stubble.

"Real money. Bro, this Ruger Crew shit tattooed on me ain't just a crew. It's a whole movement. We make bosses out of niggas, young bosses, might I add. The grandfather of the movement, Dallas, ain't but twenty-four and he's already been retired for over a year. And his baby brother, Sean... my lil hellraiser, has spread his wings and branched out in places like Atlanta and Miami, while Lil Ronnie and I got the city on lock back home. And you can't even get close to Lil Ronnie without going through me. I'm telling you... I can open doors." Monte looked at 200 seriously. "And I can open that mufucka right up for you."

200 saw a fire in Monte that he knew couldn't be fake. He actually believed what he said about there was real money to be made. And with less than seven days left before PG would wash his hands, what other choice did he have? He took a deep breath, then extended his hand. "Well," he said solemnly, "looks like I'ma St. Lunatic now."

Chapter 15

A ferocious bark, coupled with the rattling of the fence, momentarily spooked Jaylen as he walked through the night cold of Highland Hills. He looked at the fence and saw the gleam of the snarling dog's teeth. But knowing the aging Rottweiler was a mutt, he didn't even respond. The handsome prep star embodied a different feng shui, so to speak. He was fresh off a movie date with this fine upperclassman who had him feeling like he signed his first NFL check. It sucked that his phone was lost, and he couldn't give the bro the rundown. But after seeing 200's dusty Tahoe outside of their moms' house, he couldn't wait to brag that he went past first base. He patted his lower neck, hoping she didn't leave a hickey. He could hear his brother now complaining about how he broke all the player rules.

Reaching inside his blue varsity letterman jacket, Jaylen retrieved the key to the modest brick home. He thought nothing of it that the door was unlocked. He was too busy smiling mischievously, wondering how 200 would tease him if he found a mark. But upon entering the home, then seeing 200 covered in blood, sorrow struck him like he'd been blindsided by a reckless car. The troubled look. The vibe. For as far back as he could remember, his mother's home never had this energy. Something wasn't right.

"Jason, what's wrong? Wh-where's Mom?" Jaylen stuttered.

The way 200 shook his head didn't ease his worries. In fact, it instigated them further. Jaylen was so busy searching his eyes, he didn't realize that he grabbed his jacket.

"Huh ... did you hear me? I said, Where's Moms?" When Jaylen saw emotion build in 200's eyes and he didn't want to answer him, he tried to go see for himself. But there was something 200 didn't want him to see. They began to wrestle. Jaylen for confirmation of his mother's well-being, and 200 to prevent his young eyes from witnessing a travesty.

"I can't let you go in there." 200 struggled to keep the young brute from entering the kitchen as his tears bounced off the hardwood floor.

At the same time, another voice seemed to wrestle its way into Jaylen's consciousness.

"Jaylen, are you coming?"

But 200's voice was too strong. "Please, bro, I can't let you see her like this."

As Jaylen struggled to get to the kitchen like a drowning person trying to get to shore, he felt someone grab his foot, waking him from the recurring dream of Renee. He blinked his eyes to coherence, to find Coach Phil standing at the post of his canopy bed. He was dressed like he was on the sidelines and smelled like the cologne aisle at Macy's.

"Wake up," Coach Phil said. "Me and Craig headed over to Fast Eddie's to grab a few burgers and fries. You coming?"

Although Fast Eddie's was one of his favorite joints, Coach Phil's question reminded him that he was without his favorite girl.

"No, I'll just stay here." Jaylen threw the comforter over his damp face, even though he was an early bird, and it was already twelve.

95

Coach Phil could sense that he was down, but didn't want to press. "Alright. Well whatever Lil Craig gets, I'll make sure he orders the same for you."

Jaylen waited for the door to click closed, before he showed any signs of life. He scooted up slightly on the oversized wooden headboard and began to stare up listlessly at the tall, pastel colored ceiling. The paint quickly turned into a sea where he conjured an image of Renee's beautiful face. A smile flickered at the corner of his mouth while an emotion-filled heat warmed his eyes.

It was still tremendously hard to cope with her death. But when it got too hard, all he could do is take Aunt Doonie's advice and pray. He closed his eyes and prayed for an escape from this pain. Prayed the killer would be brought to justice. And finally prayed his successes filled her with pride for all her days. Opening his eyes, things felt a little bit easier and he swore he heard a voice say, "It's going to be okay."

Forty-five Minutes Later

200 craned his neck to talk on the phone as he moved around the ritzy apartment with haste. He saw Queen and stopped and said something to her before getting back to his conversation.

"Yeah, Jaylen, why don't you just hit me on the FaceTime real quick? Besides, I wanna see you and that new trophy."

"You sure? You sound pretty busy. If you want, I can just hit you back."

"Don't worry 'bout that. I got this right chere."

"Okay," Jaylen said, before hanging up to pull up the app.

200 slid his phone inside his skinnies, then braced his steps for a fast-moving Queen.

"Do you want me to pack this one or this one?" Queen held up his two most expensive coats.

200 thought about the persona of a music industry manager that Monte wanted him to project in the 'Lou.

"Umm, pack 'em both." He gave her a quick smooch then headed to the kitchen where he would have some good light to FaceTime with Jaylen. Just as he was pulling a tan wooden stool from the polished island, he felt his phone vibrate. He opened the screen and wiped the sweat from his head. "Bro, what's up?"

"What are you doing?" Jaylen's fresh face furrowed.

"Packing. I'm 'sposed to be leaving for St. Louis in the morning."

"St. Louis... what are you going to St. Louis for?"

In the back of his mind, 200 knew he was making a last-ditch effort to save Jaylen's life, and essentially his own. But he downplayed the seriousness of the situation. "To help Monte with something."

Right when Jaylen was about to rhetorically repeat 200's answer, a naturally beautiful Queen walked into view, stealing the show.

"I got some of your cologne, those jewels you mentioned, and just about everything that looked winterproof," she reeled off.

"Oh, say hi to my brother." 200 grabbed Queen's hips and turned her towards his image. Queen waved hello and unintentionally wooed him with those angel eyes.

"What's up?" Jaylen asked, licking his lips. "I mean like, fo' real... what's up with me and you?" Queen blushed at his cuteness, then went to the fridge to grab a water. When 200 zoomed back in on himself, Jaylen asked with excitement, "Man, who is she to you?"

Ironically, Queen was walking past him. He grabbed her and brought her back into the frame. "Queen, who am I to you?" He looked into the depths of her eyes.

She stroked his nappy twists, then kissed his cheek. "Baby."

200 watched her lustfully as she swayed off. And when he turned, Jaylen bombarded him with questions.

"She going to St. Louis too?"

"Actually, all this stuff is not going to St. Louis. Some of it is going to her crib where, after I get my shit together, I plan to move you."

"When?"

"Maybe in a week or two," 200 confirmed.

"Nice." Although Jaylen was having fun at Coach Phil's, there wasn't anybody in this world he was closer to than 200. He wished two weeks was today. "Oh, wait. Lemme go grab the trophy for you real quick." Jaylen took off. When he came back, he was holding a beautiful gold trophy that was the size of a three-year old.

"Okay! Okay!"

"Yeah, man, in a minute we gone need a museum to house all this. We can call it Jaylen's Symposium. It can house my athletic trophies, my academic achievements, and pics of all these lil fast girls that want a player to take 'em down."

Jaylen's statement made 200 bust out laughing. He seemed to always get tickled by Jaylen's confident swag.

Seeing that he had him going, Jaylen snuck a question in. "Hey, can I get a tattoo?"

"A tattoo?" 200 sobered.

"Yeah." Jaylen looked at his forearm where he wanted it. "I want to get a dedication to Mom."

"You can get a tattoo in like two years, when you turn seventeen. Right now, just keep tattin' a legacy for yourself. Something that she would be proud of."

Queen stepped back into 200's circumference, dusting her hands. "All set."

Jaylen could see 200 preparing to end the FaceTime. "Aye, bring me some White Castle back, you hear me?"

"Some White Castle?"

"Yeah, I always wanted to try it."

"Man, by the time I get back, that shit gon' be crusty and dry."

GET IT IN SLUGS 2 | B. STALL

"I don't care. I'll still eat it. Maann, you ain't even paying attention." Hoping for a win with Queen he asked, "What about you? Can you bring me some White Castle?"

200 pulled her into him protectively. "Nah, she only get food for one dude." He kissed her neck. "And that's me."

"Forget what he talkin' 'bout. You need you a young nigga," Jaylen shot at Queen. "I can take care of you, girl. You know I'm finna get those name-and-likeness checks soon."

200 teased him even more by kissing Queen and depressing the screen black. Then after their smiles relaxed and a hint of seriousness returned to 200's face, Queen soothed both of his shoulders and asked, "You ready for your flight?"

200 nodded as he stared off listlessly. "Ready as I'll ever be." Then he felt Queen's soft hand slide inside his sweater.

"Well, what we gone do with the rest of this time?"

200's eased her hand lower. "I can think of a few things."

Chapter 16

The Next Day

Judge Lawrence Little had zero tolerance for games. After his chair squeaked and he let out a sigh of frustration, all the eyes in the courtroom seemed to focus on Mr. Daley. It was Thursday morning and his client, 200, was expected to be in court to plead out to a year for a gun charge. A fact that was exaggerated by the ticking clock on the wall, which reminded the quiet courtroom he was twenty minutes late. Mr. Daley saw the eagle-eyed glare the judge was giving him and deflected it with a faint laugh.

"He'll be here," Daley assured. He took a sip of his coffee to hide his nerves. *C'mon, Mr. Goodwin, you've got me looking like a sitting duck.*

***

Tasha saw 200 dozing in his window seat and pushed the armrest up to lay on his chest. Monte had driven his Benz back to St. Louis. And the flight wasn't overbooked, so they had the private corner next to the restroom to themselves. 200 opened his eyes briefly and saw his chocolate soldier getting comfortable. He didn't trip off her doin' her and closed his eyes and drifted back to sleep. He slumbered for what felt like eternity, but was actually three minutes, before he recognized a groan leaving her lips. Feeling the sensations, he slowly opened his eyes then looked down to find the top of Tasha's lime-green streaked head, bobbing and slurping away.

"Oh shit," 200 said in surprise as Tasha kept giving him that crazy head. She didn't even care about the possibility of someone seeing her. She just kept expressing her desire for him with each warm, saliva-filled gulp. "Damn, ma, what you doing?" he asked, but wasn't mad.

Tasha pushed his dick towards her mouth a few more times before she was able to subdue herself. "You know what we do when we want something." She twisted saliva along his length. "We take it."

"So, that's what yo pretty ass doing? You just gone take the dick?" 200 asked.

She moaned, "Yeah." But her obvious focus was on showing that work. She covered his leaning flesh with her warm mouth. And Tasha was no ordinary head doctor, she was schooled in the fine halls of Diamond Cabaret. She began to work her tongue, which was softer than silk. Then the faster her speed increased, the sloppier and louder her noises became. 200 looked around nervously. "Shhh … quiet down a bit."

Though his words didn't curb her enthusiasm, she sucked it slower and more sensually. 200 shook his head as he watched a pro at work. It wasn't fair that her head was this good. She was making his loins build with each head-twirling gulp. Unexpectedly, 200's troopers went for a dive towards the back of her throat.

"Gotdamn, Tasha. You a fool. Ain't no chick ever made me bust this fast in my life." He looked at her stunned. He let off for about as long as he lasted, two and a half minutes. But his dick did something else he wasn't used to, staying hard after he bust. Tasha stared at it as she twisted her manicured hand along his length.

"I would put this pussy on you, but I know you got a girl. And I don't want her blaming me for having your head gone."

"Girl, get yo ass up and go to the bathroom," 200 competitively objected. "I know you don't think I'm finna let you get the best of me like that."

200 wouldn't allow himself to think about Queen. Far as he knew, he wasn't promised tomorrow. He was living for today. He pressed his exposed erection into Tasha's water balloon soft ass as they hustled into the empty bathroom stall. Quickly, he turned the lock from the green side to the red occupied side. Now, it was a race to get Tasha out of them clothes.

Removing her skin-tight blue jeans was tougher work than he anticipated. But once he caught sight of her naked ass, he felt like the middle of her thighs was far enough. He began to toy with it, open it. Damn she was thick. And her kitty was fat and hung just right. He was ready to give her the business. He took his dick and teased her opening before pushing inside her resistance.

"Oh shit," she moaned.

"Damn!" 200 stopped mid-stroke. "If I woulda known that pussy was this good, I woulda been hit that shit." He began to serve her.

***

A loud gavel summoned both councils to the judge's bench. Mr. Daley tried to speak but Judge Little completely ignored him. "Alright, Prosecutor, we're going to go ahead and issue a warrant for Mr. Goodwin's arrest. And I want this to be a priority. I want him off the streets as soon as possible."

"Will do." Zellers flashed a knowing grin before she walked off to tend to the task.

But Mr. Daley didn't give up. He was still protesting on his client's behalf. "C'mon, Your Honor. Don't be so presumptuous. Can't you just reschedule for a later date? A different time, maybe?"

"You're obviously not privy to the threat your client poses to the community. We gave him a chance to appear in court. Now we'll leave it in the cops' hands."

Judge Little turned in his robust chair to tend to other matters, dismissing Daley like he was a bum on the corner, instead of a high-powered attorney.

Chapter 17

"So, is it always this cold?" Tasha stared out of Monte's Benz at the snow flanked streets of St. Louis.

"Actually, it's not really that bad. The snow is melting, and the sun is expected to be in the forecast for the rest of this week."

Tasha shook her head and pouted in the most alluring way. "I guess." Then they continued to proceed from the airport back to the expensive home Monte rented.

As landmarks passed in front of them, and they made a special stop for 200, they made small talk, mainly about the unexpected turn of events at the game room. 200 told him how the news reported that the raid was conducted by rogue cops. That they might be in the clear. And in the midst of Tasha admitting this was one of the reasons she wanted to relocate, the car slowed in front of Monte's Hazelwood home.

The trendy two-story looked like one of those vacation homes you might rent off Airbnb. His old school was in the garage, so he parked the Benz in the salt dried driveway. After looking at the twenty-yard trip to the glass screen door with trepidation, Tasha hopped out and everyone else followed suit.

"Dang," Tasha said, walking swiftly, making her soft curves bounce. "That's what I get for tryna be cute. I knew I shoulda brought a heavier coat."

Monte couldn't help but laugh. These two southerners probably never veered this far north, let alone in the winter. He was willing to bet they never felt wind with this much bite.

"Yes, it gets cold in the 'Lou, it ain't like Texas." He let them inside. "'Round here, you gotta buy winter clothes... gloves, scarfs, heavy coats and all that."

After placing some luggage in the closet, they all found comfort in different quarters of the tastefully furnished living room. Monte looked over at 200 who was mowing down some White Castle cheese fries.

"Damn, you must have been starvin' or something."

200 looked at Tasha knowingly. "Yeah, I worked up a lil appetite. But this shit good. No wonder Jaylen wants me to bring some back."

"Man, that ain't even scratchin' the surface when it comes to the food that we known for. Now I wish I had time to really show y'all around. But you know we gotta get down to business. Did you bring the jewels?"

200 wiped his greasy hands with a napkin, then went and retrieved a small black bag from one of the suitcases in the closet. He emptied the suede bag on the table like how the guys in the movies do a cache of precious diamonds. There was his personal collection, the jewels they were paid to take from C.T. Shiesty, even the pieces they got off of Fooley Wayne and his squad.

"Now this looks like something straight outta the rapper's closet on *Cribs*," Monte examined the jewels. "Put 'em on."

"Huh?"

"Put 'em on," Monte urged.

Confused but compliant, 200 draped himself in jewels. Then as he was about to put on the last piece, Monte abruptly stopped him.

"Hold on, I'ma put this right here on Tasha." He grabbed C.T. Shiesty's sparkling diamond choker. Then he backed up, exuding the mannerisms of a photographer before stopping. "That's it! That'll do it! Now you can officially pass for Fooley Wayne's manager, and you Ms., are his newest signee."

Tasha began to check her fresh with the jewels on. "Oh, I'm liking this already." But 200 began to remove his, as he looked a tad bit sour.

"I still don't get it. How is this supposed to help us get closer to Lil Ronnie's riches?"

"It's not gone help us get close to Lil Ronnie's riches. It's the only way we get close to Lil Ronnie's riches, trust me. He's game tight, and I'd probably do better tryna get y'all near the Pope. Approaching him, we'll have to implore a little more finesse. And I told you I could get that door open for us, and this is how we do it. Lil Ronnie longs to be like his Ruger Crew predecessors and start a legal business. So, he followed his passion for music and started an indie label. He's got a roster of rappers, and some of them niggas is really poppin'. But he can't get this trap shit out of his system long enough to give them the attention their talent deserves. Instead, he uses his studio more like a stash house. I know. I done been around and watched him secure a million cash."

"A mil'?" 200 responded.

"Yep, more than once. There's always money stashed there, and I can count on one finger how many times I done seen some moved. Now, what we need to do is bait Lil Ronnie into believing we're his missing link into the music industry. Get him to invite us to the studio. And from there, it'll be like a pig walking into its own slaughter."

Monte saw that 200 was the only one that wasn't excited.

"Don't worry, Cuz, the play is solid. We just need a few days to build a rapport."

200 continued to show dread. "I'm not sure I have that type of time. In four days, PG is gonna make good on his threats if I don't come through with his money."

"Say no more. Lemme get on the ball." Monte started towards his phone. "I talked to him earlier. Lemme see if he made it down this way." Monte pressed dial as he ducked into the kitchen to get some privacy. But unbeknownst to Tasha and 200, he hadn't spoken to Lil Ronnie yet. The pressure of him having his people fly in seemed to make this call more intense. He couldn't think of the possibility of his plan falling through. He just needed Lil Ronnie to answer. His foot tapped with increased fervor with each passing ring.

***

The professional hands of a masseuse dug into Lil Ronnie's dark tatted shoulders, while another set of hands used a rock to knead the balls of his feet. *This is what being a king must feel like*, thought Lil Ronnie as he laid across the padded table of a preferred Crestwood massage parlor. It was another attempt for the twenty-five-year-old to become more cultured, and he found the whole scenery and ambiance to be refreshing. As he teetered on the verge of sleep, his phone vibrated for the umpteenth time. It didn't seem to bother him, but it was driving one attractive Vietnamese masseuse half-crazy.

She set the therapy rock down then walked around a vibrantly colored partition and came back seconds later with his denim jeans in her outstretched arm.

"Lay dien thoai nay!" loud words left her little lips.

Lil Ronnie couldn't understand what she said, though he knew she meant business. The more Americanized and slightly thicker one grabbed his pants, then paraphrased her coworker's grievance. "Can you please turn your ringer off?" Lil Ronnie pressed it to silence, then answered the call coming in from Monte.

"Hello… whoa, slow down, cowboy. Yeah, I've heard of Fooley Wayne. The lil D-town rappa that got shit crackin'." As Lil Ronnie listened to his hitta explain their connection, he gradually thought, *I mighta been wrong about lil buddy.* He saw Monte as a knucklehead with potential, who had a hard time listening. But now he was presenting an outlet that could help him further his music venture and doing so with the eloquence of a boss. "And this is your peoples?" he asked Monte. "Yes, I can help you show 'em a good time. Let's do Farmhaus. It's a five-star restaurant. I know they'll like that. Alright, cool. That's what's up. I'll meet y'all there around 8:00."

After Lil Ronnie hung up, the masseuse quickly brought him back to his royal treatment. "Everything okay?" she asked in her pleasant dialect.

"Actually," Lil Ronnie said as he sat upright, "things could be better." He opened his white towel then looked down at the impressive print in his dark trousers. "Do you massage everything?" He already knew the answer. That was code word for more "fun." The sexy Vietnamese women looked at each other then laughed. Then they slowly eased towards Lil Ronnie with a different therapy in mind.

***

Lil Ronnie didn't expect to hit it off with Monte's people the way he did. But after a robust dinner in an exclusive setting, and some surprisingly good conversation, he nodded at 200 in admiration. The industry big shot had a presence about himself and a way with words that seemingly saved their night right off the bat. From the hours of 5:00 to 8:00, Farmhaus was known to have an extensive line, but he smoothed things out with a random waitress and got them seated right away.

It was there where he learned Tasha, the diamond princess with them, was 200's new artist. How 200 elevated from the streets to the boardroom. And 200's affinity for style. The man could dress. With a collar of faux fur on his Italian designer coat, and gaudy gold glasses, 200 looked like 21 Savage on his way to the Met Gala. Lil Ronnie liked to dress himself, but this made him want to take some racks and revamp his whole wardrobe.

As Monte aimed his phone to get an Instagram pic of all this excess food and elaborate china, the white waitress came back to the table with a smile and their eight-hundred-dollar bill. 200 slid it by him before somebody could object, then texted a few more characters in his phone before fetching his credit card.

"Obligations," 200 said to Lil Ronnie, looking up from his phone as if he was hard at work when he actually was just checking on Queen and Jaylen.

"Industry business?"

"What else?"

"You seem to be balancing a lot of that."

200 nodded demurely. "I stay busy… I can't front. I just try to work smart and not hard though. The secret is hiring the smartest people at what they do. I manage them and in turn, we bring out the best opportunities for our artists."

"Nice. I mighta learned something today," Lil Ronnie said.

But not nearly as much as 200. For the better half of the day, 200 was online studying hip-hop managers. Their look. Their lingo. All in an attempt to be better prepared for any scenario he might face. He'd even Cashapp'd the waitress beforehand to reserve a table. He was pulling out all the stops. He wanted this nigga bad.

After the waitress charged 200's card for the bill and her generous tip, Monte began to rub his hands together. "So, what's up? The night going too good to end it now. I say we hit up one of those strip clubs over there in my hood on the Eastside."

"Our hood," Lil Ronnie seconded.

"The hood-hood. The hell you talkin' 'bout. Can't have them coming through the 'Lou without crossing that bridge to the *Ill side*," he said, referring to East St. Louis, Illinois.

200 downed the rest of the wine then stood. "Sheit, we fuck with the hood too. You ain't said nothing but a word."

***

A concert of doors slammed as they hopped out of different model Benz's beneath the neon lighting outside of Club Onyx. Everyone in the group except Tasha had decided to shed their coat, flashing their jewelry proudly, maybe even boldly, considering where they were. This part of East St. Louis, with its backdrop of strip clubs nestled within a jungle of poverty-stricken homes, was known to be the most cutthroat. Even a guerilla like 200 picked up on the vibe.

"You got yo unit?" he asked Monte.

"Unit? Nigga, we are a unit. A nigga try this Ruger Crew shit don't be surprised if you see security bussin' for us. But to answer yo question, yeah, I got it. Me and Lil Ronnie."

With his head on a swivel, 200 followed them to the entrance. Then his paranoia began to wane as they bypassed the line and security greeted Monte 'nem as if they were kinfolks. They did the procedural pat down, but it was all for show. It was obvious they fucked with the Ruger Crew strong. After some more fake love from security, they followed the growing bass inside and were greeted by raining money and ass and titties.

"Oh! That's what I'm talkin' 'bout. Work, bitch!" Tasha urged, seeing a pretty-skinned diva percolating against a pole. She was dancing on a stage made of all fixtures that glowed white with some pink and soft blues. "This is nice," Tasha gushed.

"Yeah, prolly cause you here," Monte whispered in her ear. "All bullshit aside, ma, you the baddest thang in this club."

Tasha's lime-green ponytail whipped around as she looked back. "You just saying that."

"Just saying that? I don't have to say it, everybody could see it. You got this black jumpsuit on that got niggas thinking 'bout a way in it, plus you rockin' the matching fur with all this ice that got you looking like a million-dollar bitch. No offense, that is."

A smile began to form on her adorable chocolate face. "None taken."

Breaking their spell, Lil Ronnie nudged Monte and invited him to come with the guys and change out some bills. They came back to where she stood a song and a half later and were surprised to see Tasha holding a stripper's arm up as she twirled her around to show off her bangin' body. Tasha had the cutest smile as she nodded in approval.

"Yeah, you definitely ready. Now go up there and get that money." She smacked her on her dimpled ass. Monte smacked her on the ass too.

"Yeah, get that money." Then he immediately began tossing ones from his blocks of cash.

Seeing some connection, 200 asked Tasha, "Who was that?"

Tasha hunched her shoulders. "Yo guess as good as mine." But with Lil Ronnie within earshot, she didn't wanna say she knew her from a club back in Dallas. She wasn't Tasha the stripper right now. She was Tasha the rapper. Even Quavo's "Strub Da Ground" and her girl's playful urging couldn't get her on stage. Then she heard all the masculine pleading from the guys standing around and noticed the racks in their hands, and her stripper instincts kicked in. "Fuck it. Lemme give 'em a lil taste," she told herself. And from the minute her heels touched the stage, she began to perform.

Tasha's moves were sultry and fluid. She didn't have to break a sweat to get niggas reeling. She looked like a top-notch chick losing her inhibitions for her man. Locking eyes with some of the dudes in front of the stage, she began to adlib Yung Miami's part when she said, "Expensive as hell and worth it." Then she turned around and showed the crowd exactly what she meant. She looked back as she popped one cheek, making her fur move. Then the right one. Now the left one, until she was sending the crowd into a frenzy. She felt bills rain, even some rolls and unabashedly put them in her top. Then she made her ass roll a few more times until she felt like they'd seen enough.

Niggas was begging her to get back on stage and had she been back at Diamond Cabaret, she would've gotten that money. She stepped over to the crew. And while they were fanning her off after the hot performance, her girl rushed over with a handful of bills, saying, "This for you." Tasha eyeballed the money, nodding her head. In one verse, she'd made close to five racks.

Over the course of an hour, Tasha used some of that money to buy her guys bottles. The vibe was liberated, and they were bringing new girls to the stage. But 200 felt like if he was to stay true to his role, it was best if they left now. He leaned over to Lil Ronnie.

"I'ma get going."

"Already?"

"Yeah, all this traveling gave me a lil 'lag. Plus, it's past 2:00 and I got a conference call at eight in the morning. But hopefully we can get up before I leave so you can show me some more of the city."

"No doubt," Lil Ronnie assured.

200 shook Lil Ronnie's hand, hoping they made a connection, but ready to say fuck Monte's plan and fast forward the bullshit.

Chapter 18

Back In Texas the Next Day

"So, you would really kill the kid?" McGraw asked PG as they were pulling bricks of coke out the floor at PG's dilapidated factory.

"Let the nigga not come with the money, and we gon' find out."

McGraw looked up with those tiger green eyes. "But what if he do?"

"What if he do? Humph. I never thought about that. Then I'll prolly have Jaylen kill 200. Yeah, that'll do it. Make the lil brother dome the big brother. Maybe that'll be retribution for 200 killing Buck and Mia."

"Fool, you crazy." McGraw shook his head then went back to preparing the shipment they were forced to front to their peoples out in Chicago.

Since PG never gave Slick the money to square off the connect, Slick cut him off, forcing him to shop with an inferior plug. This was one of the many hardships he attributed to 200, which had him giving his idea some serious thought.

***

For much of the day, 200 was on pins and needles dreading that they'd missed their opportunity to get at Lil Ronnie. Now that it was 5:00 and he finally heard Monte returning, he stared at the door with expectant eyes, hoping for a change in plans.

Monte took one step inside and stopped in his tracks. "The fuck is this?" 200 had an assault rifle at his side and looked more like a street soldier ready to pull a caper, than he did a street nigga turned industry executive.

Tasha sat forward. "I told him that he was gonna drive himself crazy. But he's been stressing about this lick ever since you left."

"Stressing? You call this stressing? I just want to get shit in motion. You try being patient when the most important person in your world's life is being threatened."

"Look… chill, dawg." Monte tossed a bookbag with his block earnings aside. "You might as well put the weapon back up, because I told you we ain't gettin' at Lil Ronnie till tomorrow."

"You told me?" 200 frowned as if the words tasted acid leaving his lips.

"Yeah, I told you, 200. For the hundredth time, we gotta get him comfortable enough to invite us to the studio."

"Man, fuck that. I say we put that steel in his life and make this whole process a lil bit faster."

Monte shook his head. "That's not your call to make." But he understood the thirst of an unfed jack boy and tried to take a more subtle approach. "Look, let me break it down like this. Gettin' at Lil Ronnie is like hunting deer. You gotta bait him in with a sense of calm and get him to come to us. Right now, he trusts us and everything is going as planned. But the minute we start pressing him about getting up with us sooner, it's gon' raise his radar. Next thing you know, he gone have a bunch of niggas tagging along on the move, which is gone lead to a lot of unnecessary bloodshed."

But 200 still wasn't hearing it.

"Then what the fuck you invite me for? Cause making shit bleed is what I do."

Seeing 200 fuming mere inches from Monte's face, Tasha said, "Y'all chill."

But Monte didn't back down. It wasn't in his blood. "I invited you cause I needed an outsider who was official. It could be deadly if word got back to the crew that I had my hand in this. Not cause I need you running my lick. Trust me, fam." He placed a calming hand on 200's shoulder. "We on the same page. I'ma help you get this money for Jaylen. And I'ma get an enemy out the way. Just curb that energy for one more day. And in the meantime, use some of that 200 smarts to help us on this lick."

Monte patted him on the shoulder again and assured they were gon' hit the play. And while his face showed confidence, 200 still had his worries.

Chapter 19

The very next day, having texted Lil Ronnie to link up, Monte avoided calling him again and spent the rest of the time wondering if he would get back. It was 6:40 now on his stainless-steel refrigerator and he was stressing like 200 was the other day. He knew 200 only had two days left to pay PG and it would be a catastrophe if his plans were to fall through.

Ashing a blunt, Monte saw 200 walking towards him at his alcohol decorated wet bar. "What you smiling about?" he asked, seeing the phone in his hand.

200's smile seemed to reach his beady eyes. "I'm on my best shit on this one. I got the nigga Fooley Wayne in on the Lil Ronnie play."

"Fooley Wayne? Nah. How'd you do that?"

"I told him that if he wasn't by the phone to FaceTime when I called, I would release the tape of him getting robbed *immegiately.*"

"*Immegiately?*"

"*Immegiately,*" 200 reiterated. "I gave him the rapper-manager rundown. And he was damn near ready to stay on the line the whole time."

"That was genius. I knew you'd bring something extra to the table."

"Sheit, if that's the case, then you should gimme an extra cut, split this bitch fifty-fifty with the kid."

"Fifty-fifty? Damn. you tryna cut me all the way out the box. I took a big chance on this one. It could be just enough to cover Jaylen's ransom, or it might be 'mo. But either way, the rest, going to me. I done hit all these licks for lil cuz off GP, but if shit hits the fan, then I gotta deal with the consequences. You gotta respect the game." Monte flipped a plait out of his face.

200 extended his tatted hand. "Respect. But you can't blame a nigga for trying."

"Not at all."

They shared a laugh before 200 brought up the more pressing matter.

"So, what's up with Lil Ronnie?"

In the nanosecond that Monte contemplated, dread erupted inside him. He didn't want to tell 200 he hadn't gotten back, and he was worried like he was yesterday that the plan might not manifest. He really didn't know what to tell him to buy his patience. But before he spoke, Tasha rushed in with his loud ringing phone in her pampered hand.

"Here."

Monte saw it was the lil thot he banged in Texas and pressed ignore. He did a good job masking the disappointment on his aggressive-looking dark face.

"So?" 200 persisted. "What's up? What he say?"

"Look…" Just as Monte was about to deliver bad news, his phone rang again. Only this time, he was happy to see the caller. "Lil mufuckin' Ronnie, what's good?" Monte waited as he replied. "Nah, they ain't left. We out here in Hazelwood. 200 in there wrapping up a conference call and Tasha walking around looking good enough to eat." Monte listened again as contentment flashed in his eyes. "Hell yeah, I think they'll like Legacy too. Matter of fact, pull the Eurus out. Might as well send them off with a bang." After hearing what time, Monte hung up with a brimming smile.

"Everything good. We all set. He say he'll be through around ten. So y'all need to start pulling that high dollar shit out and get back in that role."

"You gotta large coin?" Tasha asked Monte.

"Coin? What kinda random ass question is that?"

"Trust me. Just find one. It's gone come in handy."

***

Kameisha walked around the mini mansion she shared with Lil Ronnie, with her arms folded across her black nightie and her bottom lip poked out. If any man were to see that adorable pout on her cute, freckled face, they would be breaking their neck trying to see what's wrong and she would have gladly told them. The twenty-six-year-old, who's known Lil Ronnie since he was a snotnose, and who's been exclusively his for the past three years, felt the father to be, couldn't be trusted. She had heard every excuse in the book when it came to his promiscuous ways. *I was out of town on business. Something came up with the load. She was only at the spot because of one of the guys. And now I'm politicking with an industry executive.*

Again?

Kameisha initially believed him because he spoke with such conviction about what this meant for the label, saying this was a once in a lifetime opportunity. But then she read the clock by their oversized bed and smacked her lips. At eleven o'clock. *Industry executive, my ass.*

To try to curb her insecurities, Kameisha rested her shapely posterior on the even softer down comforter and tried to relax. She hadn't heard recent gossip about Lil Ronnie's cheating. But this was still Lil Ronnie, a version of ASAP Rocky in St. Louis. Could she fully trust him to do right?

Swooping her long natural braids over her shoulder, Kameisha rested against the bed's padded headboard. She began to focus on the show that was in progress on Starz. But after about fifteen minutes, the Tempur-Pedic mattress started to get the best of her. Her eyes grew heavier and heavier. And just as she fell into a sleep-like state, she was jolted from it when Lil Ronnie's business phone vibrated like a drill on the nightstand.

Kameisha grabbed the glowing Samsung Galaxy. It had an alert that showed someone had arrived at Lil Ronnie's discreet tan brick studio. He had gotten this app installed to keep watch of the studio's precious cargo. Not the new equipment he bought, but the one point eight mil he had stashed inside. This wasn't above Kameisha's pay grade. She wasn't just a pretty face. This was Lil Ronnie's thug. She played a vital role in the lick that put him on out west, so he knew she could handle being his second set of eyes.

Once the headlights went out, she was able to make out the silhouette of Lil Ronnie's midnight black Lambo truck. *Mm-hmm. Let's see what kind of executive shit this nigga really got going on,* she thought. She perched up and watched the footage closer. Then as a broad stepped out the truck with lime-green hair, wearing a short black dress with too many cutouts for this weather, she shook her head. She really couldn't stand no woman around her man. But seconds later, two well-dressed men stepped out, which made her simmer down. *Hmm. Maybe he is entertaining industry people.*

One of the men looked like Lil Ronnie's trusted capo, Monte. But it was hard to tell with the poor lighting that surrounded the studio. The camera followed them inside and she was about to urge him to take care of his business, when suddenly, someone stepped behind Lil Ronnie and hit him in the back of the head with a pistol. He followed with more vicious blows.

"Unt-uh. Hell nawl! Stop fuckin' hitting my baby!"

Kameisha ran to her phone and called a leader in the Ruger Crew.

"Y'all need to mount up and meet me at the studio," she said frantically. "These niggas is tryna kill Lil Ronnie."

***

Tasha dug into the scalp of Lil Ronnie's dreads and brought his bloody face off the floor as he groaned like a wounded animal. The last blow from Monte's pistol had knocked him out cold, giving them time to strip him down to his boxers and restrain his hands and feet.

This was a moment, just hours ago, they fretted wouldn't happen. Then, Lil Ronnie scooped them up and things started to play out. He watched 200 discuss an itinerary with Fooley Wayne on FaceTime, which opened his eyes to how much work it took to play at this level of the game.

Later on the trip, he heard Tasha adlibbing the lyrics she texted into her phone. And when she'd requested that they hit the nearest studio instead of the club, he'd offered his, hoping to get in good for his label. Too bad Tasha couldn't rap a lick and the industry insider that impressed him was actually a notorious jack boy.

"Is it sinking in yet that we mean business?" Tasha challenged.

"Is what sinking in? That you think I'm coming off my money? You got me fucked up."

Monte stepped forward. "Nah, you got us fucked up and you really gone find out if you keep tryna drag this out."

"Monte, fuck you. You think I'm scared of you cause you got a lil shiny pistol? You been wanting my spot. You just been too much of a girl to take it. Go 'head, shoot. Shoot, muthafucka. Shoot!" he dared. "Just what I thought, straight pussy. And you..." He glared over at 200. "What the fuck you over there all quiet for?"

200 was posted against the wall studiously searching Lil Ronnie's phone as if the brutal scene wasn't even playing out before him. Lil Ronnie hawked some blood-filled phlegm at

him to tell him fuck him too. That was the last thing he remembered before everything around him went black. He woke up minutes later with a throbbing headache and was surprised that only his left eye opened. Still, he felt defiant and wanted to give them hell. That was until 200 finally opened his mouth to speak.

"Okay. I found his pregnant girlfriend through this locator app. She's in a neighborhood called um... Ladue. At 1021 Bell Park Drive. I say we go and get her and let him make a decision. Which one he loves most, his money or his girl?" 200 knew from Lil Ronnie's text that he was crazy about his girl. "C'mon, Tasha. Monte, you stay here while we go out here and snatch her up."

Lil Ronnie lasted all of a step and a half before he caved in like cracked wood. "No... no... no... no! Just wait. Chill," he pleaded, but Monte took offense.

"I don't know what the fuck we chillin' for. You still ain't said where you moved the money. So, we might as well swoop up Kameisha and see what that pressure does to her."

"Money? What money, Monte? That was before you went to Texas. I don't keep money like that at the studio no more."

"The hell you don't. You know what, fuck it," Money spazzed. "Y'all go 'head and grab the girl." He kicked the wind out of lil Ronnie. "I got this shit right here."

As shoes skidding and keys jingling made a soundtrack towards the door, Lil Ronnie tapped his forehead on the hardwood a few times before yelling, "Okay. I'll tell you." He then mumbled something about the restroom.

"Where!" they all yelled.

"In the restroom. Just pull the sink and cabinet out from the wall," he pronounced much clearer.

The fellas dashed through the poorly lit studio, leaving more-than-capable Tasha to stand guard. The studio looked nothing like Fooley Wayne's super plush setting. But it was a front for Lil Ronnie, trappin' is what he does. Following the warped tile flooring, Monte led them to the rear door, where an "Out of Order" sign was posted to ward people off. If that didn't work, then the smell of piss and ammonia when you stepped inside would. Though, it didn't faze Monte and 200. They were on a money mission.

Monte ripped down the yellow tape from around the sink. While 200 stroked his chin, studying the sink's layout. It took him but a second to realize that he needed to pull the sink out from where the wallpaper came up. Then he went and unhinged it so skillfully, it was like he had set it in place before. Where the sink partition once was, there was now a sizable hole in the wall, revealing two large black duffle bags.

"Well, I'll be damn!" Monte shook his head.

"You think it's money in there?" he asked.

"Best believe it is."

But still they went to check.

They pulled both bags out. Monte lifted a block of hundreds from one, and 200's heart began to thump when he saw the same. It felt like he had discovered new oil. He felt relief and contentment. He would finally be able to pay PG. As he pictured being in front of PG's smug face, he heard what sounded like a coin hitting the ground.

"Tasha, you iight in there?" 200 asked.

There was a slight commotion before she responded, "I'm good. Did y'all find everything?"

"Yeah."

"Well, y'all need to hurry up and c'mon."

They spent another two or three minutes making sure they didn't leave anything behind. Then they hustled, as fast as the bags allowed, to the sitting room where Tasha was guarding Lil Ronnie. 200 noticed Tasha wiping off a bloody knife. And there was the silver dollar she'd asked Monte for by her heel.

"What's with the coin?" 200 asked.

"I gave him an option, silver or lead. And when he couldn't make his mind up, I made it up for him." Tasha took one final look at the dead body before reminding, "Let's get going. We've been in this bitch long enough as it is." Making their way to the door, Tasha reached for it but alarmingly, the gold knob began to twist. They hurled the bags and upped their pistols before they landed. And when the people on the other side barged in, they had their weapons drawn too.

"Monte," Kameisha started. "I don't know what you call yourself doing. But my baby better be okay, and those bet not be his bags."

Monte ignored the threat coming from her petite frame. And seeing that most of the gangstas with her were Ruger Crew souljas, he placed his pistol down and urged everybody to do the same. "Y'all chill. Everybody stand down." No one budged. "Just give me a second to talk," he insisted, searching both sides.

"I don't know what you need to talk for. Ain't nothing to talk about. 'Specially if you not explaining what happened to Lil Ronnie." She raised a brow when she caught Tasha mugging. "Problem, bitch?"

The tension between their outstretched arms was at a fever high pitch. Bullets seemed seconds away from flying. Monte had to do something.

"Now look, this what this is and this how this gone go. Lil Ronnie's dead. I made a play for the spot that rightfully belongs to me. And if you ain't riding with this new Ruger Crew shit, let that be known now." He searched their hearts with his eyes. "Desi... Kerwin... Fat-Fat..."

Having their pistols aimed at Monte felt like aiming it at their brother. One by one, they all went to Monte's side until Kameisha was by herself.

"Nah, fuck that. Y'all ain't finna do my nigga like that." Kameisha mashed the trigger, nipping Fat-Fat's ear. And she was about to let her bullets rain, before a bullet from Tasha caught her in the edges of her baby hair.

"I think we better leave," Tasha said. "Unless y'all tryna go to jail."

They left the scene how it was and darted off.

Three Hours Later

Tasha entered Monte's living room after a long shower, wearing only an oversized maroon sweater as if she was at home around her man. When 200 saw her noticeable lime-green hair, he pushed a pile of money across the sectional.

"That's for you," 200 said.

Tasha gasped like it was a wedding ring and brought her hands to her mouth, inadvertently exposing her pretty panties. "For me?"

"Yeah…" 200 reached in his pocket, "…and these too." In addition to the quarter-mil he dropped on her, he tossed the keys to Lil Ronnie's Lambo truck. "Just make sure that when we get back, you get this bitch chopped."

Normally, 200 would have kept the lion's share of his eight hundred thousand-dollar cut. But since his incident with the Twinz, he wanted to show that he could be generous to his peoples.

"Oh, my God. this is crazy." She rushed over to him and began to plant short kisses wherever they landed.

200 turned from her smooches like a schoolboy who was too shy to accept affection. "Now don't go gettin' all mushy on me."

Monte cleared his throat. "Damn, I can't get none of that? A nigga bust down one point eight mil and can't get so much as a hug."

Tasha cooed as she stood with her arms out ready to appease him, which gave 200 a chance to duck off and call PG. He found privacy in the hall and did just that.

PG answered bluntly after a half ring. "Yeah."

"Aye, I got yo money."

"So, you got my money?" PG asked rhetorically.

"Yep. I had to come to St. Louis to get it. But I'll be headed out to Dallas in the morning."

"Well, that's funny, because you having my money, and me having my money is two different stories." PG paused for a second. "Oh, and I just noticed that it's after twelve o'clock, which means that it's your last day to get that to me. Now I suggest you get that to me before tonight at midnight. Unless you want us to start digging plots. I think Jaylen's would be the easiest to start with."

200 felt the line grow cold and saw the call had ended. He rushed back into the living room and tapped a docile Tasha.

"We need to get going."

She groggily sat up from her position on the couch, pouting. "Right now? I mean, you really wanna make a twelve-hour drive without getting any rest?"

"Say, if it'll help, I can send Desi and Kerwin with you," Monte offered. "They just dropped Fat-Fat off from getting his ear taped at the hospital. I know you could use the extra guns if you wanna start a war with PG."

"No... no... no... no! I don't want a war. I'ma pay this dude his money. I'm not risking my brother's life for nothing. Even if it costs me my own."

"That's love. I wish I had somebody who loved me like that," Tasha stated.

"Real shit," Monte seconded.

But 200 was trying to think of a way for both of them to walk out of this situation unscathed. "You right. It's gonna be a long trip. Let's try to get some rest."

Chapter 20

When 200 changed lanes in the gray rental Impala, he looked in the rearview and saw Tasha's headlights mirror his movements. 200 didn't let her sleep long before hitting the road. She'd complained about how she'd just gone to sleep, but he hadn't slept at all. Soon as she called it a night, he rushed and called Jaylen. Dealing with PG, there was always some bullshit in the game. So, he had to make sure lil bro was straight.

Jaylen said that he was good, just up watching some TV with Lil Craig and eating a midnight snack that Coach Phil brought back to the estate. This reminded 200, that after this beef shit subsided, to finally get up with Coach Phil. He had taken Jaylen in during a tumultuous two weeks. One that saw a pressed 200, concede to letting his mourning brother stay at his friend's. And even though Coach Phil and 200 had spoken a few times, and Renee and Jaylen thought highly of him, they'd still never met.

With the focus on getting the money to PG, 200 continued to travel up the interstate. The dark morning clouds had begun to brighten. And although it was cold outside, it wasn't nearly as cold as it was in the 'Lou. The next thirty miles were laden with trees, and it didn't take long for his mind to grow idle. 200 thought it was crazy that over the last month alone, three million dollars had been in his presence. The lick on Buck. The one on Lil Ronnie. But after he paid PG, he would barely have a pot to piss in. Frustrated didn't even begin to describe how this shit made him feel. Because there was one thing he knew, that if the Twinz never pulled that bitch move, he would have never been in this situation. His blood began to boil at the thought. And he found himself consumed by the events of that fateful night.

***

"Walk, nigga," 200 instructed. He poked Buck on his stocky shoulder blade with the choppa to get his feet moving. 200 seemed to wonder what type of elaborate set up Buck was going to lead them to next. He was thinking somewhere like the wall or the ceiling. But he was a little surprised that Buck led them back to the kitchen. He pointed past where Shocka had Mia hemmed up towards the stove.

"It's in the oven," Buck told them. He had prepared the bag earlier so they could take it to another spot.

Anxiously, 200 walked to the oven and opened it, discovering a large black duffle bag that weighed about sixty pounds. When he pulled it out, light dust rose as the bag dropped to the floor. He kneeled down and opened it. Hallelujah, he thought. Inside was a sea of large bills, blue and green. He zipped the bag back up, content that he was staring at a mil.

"You know, Buck, I tried to tell you before that a nigga like me had bull nuts," 200 taunted, starting towards him.

Buck mouthed the word "bull nuts" as if he was confused. But when 200 removed the mask from over his tatted face, it all started coming back. The dice games. The unspoken static between them. He stared in his eyes. He knew he was fucked.

"Say, kill the girl," 200 yelled to Shocka, who obliged by pushing his '40 into her dreads. B'ough! B'ough!

"No! We had a deal," Buck cried.

200 quieted him with a quick barrage of bullets to his body and face. Bop! Bop! Bop! Bop! Bop! He stared with a scowl as Buck's bloody body laid slumped against the fridge. "Bitch ass nigga," he spewed.

But his emotional victory was short lived because bullets began to blaze from behind him. The choppa leaped from his hand and his body lurched forward as the surprising shots continued to land. Three shots hit his back, and another grazed his neck, making him sprawl on his face against the floor a few feet away from Buck. He laid still like a possum, but he could hear everything around him.

"Man, what the... you killed the homie?" Shocka asked.

"Bro, fuck that shiesty ass nigga. Now we got the bread to ourselves."

"Yo, that's some bullshit, bro. We supposed to be a team."

"You gon' stand there and keep bitchin'? Or you gon' help me grab this money so we could leave?" Zilla asked.

***

200 found a way to loosen the grip his thoughts had on him, but he wasn't able to loosen the grip he had on the wheel. Sure, he would love to get at the Twinz, but right now he had bigger fish to fry. He had to remain focused on paying PG. He glanced at the green sign along the interstate and saw that he had about six more hours before he arrived in Dallas.

Chapter 21

200's jacket flapped open from the mild winter breeze as he stood at a 7-Eleven, filling his gas tank. It was a little after 2:00 p.m. now, and he was grateful to see the distinct skyscrapers and taste the familiar crisp air in his home town of Dallas. He began to realize now why the actress in the *Wizard of Oz* professed, "There's no place like home." These were the streets 200 knew like the back of his hand. The streets that loved, but mostly feared him. The streets that crowned him king.

200 wiped the sleep from his weary eyes, then looked over at Tasha. "What you smiling so hard about?"

Tasha responded with a hug that almost knocked him over.

"Damn. Okay." He went with it. "What's all this for?"

She kissed him on the neck. "I still can't believe what you did for me."

"Oh, it was nothing."

"Nah, it was most definitely something. And I wish I could do something to show you. Like…" An idea came to her as she twisted her finger in her lime-green ponytail.

"Like what?"

"Like kill PG. Please tell my you'll let me do it, 200. Please. Please. Please," she clasped her hands.

"Now you already know the answer to that. That shit gon' set off a war. And I won't put Jaylen in harm's way."

"I know... I know. But PG's gotta get his."

"He will, trust me," 200 insisted, curbing the conversation to keep from getting worked up. "But enough about that. What's up with you? You got all this new money now, a new attitude. It's too hot for you to stay around here. What are you gonna do?"

"I'ma take this Lambo truck to get chopped like you said. Tie up all my loose ends. Then I'm taking this Tasha show on the road."

"Oh, yeah? Where to?"

"I'm moving to Atlanta, baby. Taking this pimpin' to IG, and taking my game to anotha level." When she saw 200 chuckling, she continued. "After seeing how those dudes in the 'Lou clamored over a boss chick, I won't settle for anything less. I'ma model on IG. And if they money right, I'll model this pretty lil figure for 'em in person." She put her hand on her hip. "But they gotta be shittin' that grip out. A boss like me ain't playing no games."

"Okay, I heard that. Well bring yo bossy ass over here and come give me a hug," he squeezed her tight. "I love you, Tash. You one of the most loyal mufuckas I know."

After hearing her say, "I love you too," 200 relaxed his grip but Tasha kept clinging. She knew this was goodbye. 200 had been adamant that he was confronting PG alone, leaving her with no choice but to go her separate way. But what if this was it?

When Tasha finally let him go, 200 only glanced at her misty eyes before turning to nozzle his pump. He hopped in the car and adjusted the rearview mirror, seeing her enter the black Eurus. That was the last sight he saw of Tasha before he left the lot, preparing to get with PG.

As he drove further away from downtown and deeper into the cut, he began to formulate thoughts about how he would pay PG. His plan was to stash the money in the Aston's secret compartment, then put it in a high traffic area where he could easily blend in with pedestrians and watch PG retrieve it. There was no way in hell he was letting PG lure him into a trap. He would simply put everything in play, then hit him with the location when the ups were in his favor.

Continuing to Queen's, 200 found himself at a residential intersection where he entertained the contention he might face from PG about his plan. But he was jolted from that reverie when a white Range Rover jetted around the car at the left stop sign and out in front of him. His heart raced with wild excitement. 200 could've sworn he saw a pair of bushy beards. *I know them ain't them bitch ass Twinz*, he thought, grilling the Range. He was supposed to keep straight but instead made a right. He had to see if this was who he thought it was.

200 followed from a distance, eyes attentive on the Range like a cat following a piece of yarn. After about two minutes of maintaining their corner bending pace, they entered his stomping grounds of Highland Hills, where it became real to him that this could be the Twinz. A very distant grumble from the clouds preceded a graying sky. But it would be nothing like the storm he would rain down if he found out it was them. There was still so much unresolved emotion from having to bury his mom. An incident he attributed to his so-called day-ones for crossing him on the one point two-five mil. He could see them living it up, laughing at his expense. But he would be perfectly content with just having the last laugh.

200 sat up straight in his rental Impala. He could sense that the Twinz were headed to Zilla's baby mama's house because he had studied this area on Google Maps before. Not long ago, he was outside of Zilla's baby mama's house, stalking his return until the police flashed a light on him and

ran him off. Now seeing a U-Haul up the block, he tensed in anticipation. Each passing second drove his suspicion further home. He watched as the white Range Rover vanished against the curb in front of the U-Haul and he parked a half block away. Then just as it seemed as if they had disappeared, two men emerged, and their mannerisms spoke volumes. Their walk. Their height. Their stocky build.

200 became visibly agitated. "Yep, that's them." Thinking about their snake ass ways, he dug his Glock 21 out and dropped the clip to check it in one motion. "Damn." He watched their tan and blue Carhartt jumpsuits move closer to the home. "I ain't got but two shells. And this ain't gon be enough for the damage I'm about to inflict." From the looks of the U-Haul and their attire, they had planned on moving and 200 was determined to put a deadly stop to that.

After letting them make it for now, 200 crept off to Queen's home to load up on some more ammo. He went ahead and unlocked his phone's screen and called Queen to give her the heads up about what he wanted, the bag with the rest of his money and guns in it, and her pretty ass at the door looking good as ever. Queen was happy to hear that he was safely back and didn't let him off the line that easy. They ended up cakin' for a good twenty minutes. And when the scenery changed to homes starting in the four's, he announced, "I'm outside."

The garage door lifted as 200 grabbed the money out the trunk then hurried inside and pressed it closed. Queen greeted him on the wooden staircase with the bag he asked for and one of those outfits on that made it hard for him to focus. Only this time he did, much to her disappointment, taking the bag, then handing her a smaller one with all the jewels he'd heisted.

"Baby, go put these in the safe for me." 200 saw her shoulders fall. "Bae, just do it," he softly instructed. He could see that she was craving his affection and hated to be short. But he had to put PG's money together and catch up to the Twinz before they finished packing. Time was of the essence.

Once Queen shook off her confusion, she headed to the task, while 200 put PG's remaining money together. He wasted no time stashing it inside the Aston's secret compartment. Then he quickly went back to the bag and grabbed a fresh thirty-round clip. He felt Queen's shadow over him as she reentered the doorway.

"Why you in such a rush?" She put her hand on her hip.

200 stood then met her question with a fervent kiss, twisting her shirt to pull her into him as he slipped her his tongue. His kiss seemed to express deep sentiments inside him. First it was *need*. Then, it was love. And when he suddenly broke away and opened the garage, she felt like something was wrong.

"Where you going? You just got here."

200 stopped before entering the Aston. He just studied her for a minute. Queen was his baby. "You remember when you told me you was really down for me?"

She answered, "Yeah."

"Well, just know that this just comes with the territory." He closed the door and brought the car to a hum as he left out of the driveway.

Queen had found his departure more alarming than rude. She had an intuition he was walking into a bad situation.

***

As 200 jumped lanes, bringing the white Aston to a growl, a voice inside him said, *don't go back there.* It made him think about the fact that he was riding with PG's money. But he swept that aside like it was nothing. He wasn't letting the Twinz make it.

200 sped through a good portion of Highland Hills, until the familiar siding on Zilla's baby mama's house and the orange U-Haul truck rose in his windshield. He drove one

block closer, then rested at a stop sign. From there he spotted one twin loading a box onto the truck, and another coming out the house with a princess playhouse slung over his shoulder.

Their presence reminded him of the day he saved their lives, and they rewarded him by putting him in a position that cost Renee hers. It had him contemplating runnin' down on them like a mad man, bringing the car to a creep then shooting through his own window. But he wisely kept his composure and made a right before he blew a rare chance at revenge by being spotted out here in the open.

200 drove twelve houses down, then backed into the carport of an empty house Head was remodeling. The shade the carport added allowed him to retrieve the Glock without being noticed. Not that it was necessary. Around here, everyone knew 200 and his mother. Renee was beloved in this neighborhood. And if they saw 200 puttin' work in, they'd be secretly rooting it was for her.

200 took his phone and tucked it under the floor mat, then took a deep breath, preparing to go put that work in. He was like an athlete in the locker room getting in the zone before the game. And he was focused on one thought, hit everything moving. Placing a ballcap atop his head, he covered more of his face with a black covid mask then checked for his weapon and hopped out.

Immediately, he darted through two clusters of homes, covering two blocks, which put the U-Haul truck at the stop sign around the corner. From here, he scurried down the street which had a natural elevation to it. A passing car probably saw him creepin' and looking suspicious but it was too late for him to give a fuck, he was already in motion. He snuck behind the shrubbery at the edge of the curb, where it became apparent there was some activity inside the U-Haul's cargo area. That's when he peeped through the leaves and saw Shocka and Zilla talking.

"Man, you sure it's just a few more boxes?" Shocka wiped dust on his blue Carhartt jumpsuit.

"Just a few more," Zilla assured. "Then we could see what this good life talking 'bout," he laughed knowingly. As they were coming down the U-Haul's ramp, 200 spun from the shrubbery and hunted them down like two unassuming ducks. He hated the feeling that betrayal brought him. And it showed with the violent bang of his pistol.

F'ough! F'ough! F'ough!

He ran closer and caught Shocka's body before it hit the ground. More deafening slugs rocked his vulnerable ear and head.

F'ough! F'ough!

Just a few feet away, 200 heard groaning and he almost smiled, seeing Zilla trying to get up. His shadow appeared on the concrete as he loomed over him. Seeing blood only ignited his legendary temper.

"Remember me?" 200 asked, making Zilla freeze at his voice. It was said revenge was the sweetest joy, but this was an altogether greater feeling. Zilla was the one who switched sides and crossed him on the Buck lick. If it wasn't for him, who's to say if his family would have endured all this turmoil? Zilla fought onto his back and desperately copped a fruitless plea.

"Come on, dawg… It ain't like that… You know we go back." 200 nodded in agreement, met his eyes, then gave him the exact sympathy their friendship deserved—absolutely none.

A shot exploded against Zilla's head, sending 200 into a trance. He wasn't even aware of the countless shells ejecting or the tires screeching from a passing car. But he needed to snap back before he got in a wreck. Fortunately, he did when the gun's clip emptied to a click. He backpedaled a few steps as he studied the docile body, then took off towards his car in a full sprint.

Chapter 22

With all the time that PG spent on the go, he still found time to spend with Sabrina, the mother of his expectant child. He watched her stacked T-shirt clad body leave the kitchen, holding a salad that she had delivered before she knew PG was coming over. When PG summoned for what she was carrying, she raised an arched brow which revealed her confusion.

"Umm, I thought that ranch upset your stomach."

"It do. So, don't look all defensive. I want that other thing in your hand, your phone."

Sabrina plopped on the stylish white couch next to him. "Here we go. What do you want my phone for now, PG?"

"Definitely not to see if you been in contact with 200," he shot that slug. "I just wanna check Mia's Facebook page. Today's her birthday."

Sabrina deflected PG's comment about 200 like she wasn't studdin' him then pulled up the app and passed him her phone. She knew that PG didn't keep a Facebook page, because he thought it was a fed trap, and she wanted to distract him from what he was getting at. What did he know? As a smile began to form under his neatly groomed beard,

Sabrina's smile began to match his before Lil Jason's cries made her leave the room.

PG continued to scroll Mia's heavily followed page, stopping on all the enamoring photos she was tagged in. One showed her on a spring break trip he sponsored to Caicos. Another showed her with her girls at a super-lit TSU homecoming event. There was even one showing dozens and dozens of flower arrangements around her headstone. People gravitated to Mia. It was similar to the way they did their father. Mia seemed to embody his best characteristics. It was probably why he was so protective of her.

PG's sigh quivered through his chest as he tightly gripped the phone. He wondered if 200 loved Jaylen the way he did Mia. Because right now, he'd just lost the last remnant of his father, and he was looking for a void to fill it.

* * *

Adolescent laughter came up through 200's vision of killing PG, shaking him back to the soothing cabin of his Aston and the crowded parking lot of Town East Mall. 200 was fresh off a risky detour, where he deadened the Twinz. And now that he was in go-mode, it was hard to turn off. Not that he really wanted to anyhow. Killing PG was the option he favored, to calling him here to pick up the money. He would much rather make a spectacle out of his death, then passively watch from the food court as PG grabbed the cash. He knew PG's murda game couldn't match his. But at the end of the day, he knew who he was doing this for. PG would eventually get his.

200 took a deep breath, then got back focused on paying PG the remainder of his cash. A woeful feeling arose as he pressed buttons into his phone. But it wasn't all bad, the main thing was he was ensuring Jaylen's safety. 200 had two more of PG's digits to dial when out of his peripheral he saw an

alarming reflection on a car. It happened faster than an eagle swooped down on its prey.

"Police, don't move! Don't move!" the swarming officers warned, watching 200's hand slip to his waist.

200's worst nightmare was coming true. "No… no." He shook his head. "What about Jaylen?" he pleaded as if they'd knew. He looked at all the officers surrounding the car as tears filled his eyes. It didn't seem like the most rational thing, but he was ready to buck. He couldn't let anything happen to Jaylen.

Chapter 23

The Next Day

Slick entered PG's pallet recycling company, concerned as to why he couldn't reach him. He sported a designer turtleneck, expensive shoes, and that signature mystique that made him, him. He began to knock on PG's office door to announce his presence but paused, stumbling upon a weighty conversation. As more of the private conversation reached Slick's ears, he nervously scanned the hallway. He knew his integrity could be questioned for being caught in this compromising position. But still he brought his ear to the dilapidated door.

"So, your sources are saying there's more to my father's murder that meets the eye?" a curious PG asked.

"Correct. There was a DPD officer that wanted to investigate the matter. But he was transferred to another unit," informed a new voice.

"See, I knew it." PG clapped his hands. "I knew it."

The mention of his father could only mean one thing, that this was the private investigator PG had looking into the matter. Slick barged into the room, asserting his presence. "Knew what? That your father wouldn't like the way you're handling your street dealings? And that you're losing control and not focused?" Slick turned his glare from PG to the private investigator. "Excuse us." he folded his file for him. "We thank you for coming, but maybe you could continue this another time." The investigator uttered an objection, but Slick dismissed him again. "Again, thank you. But you can go now."

As the P.I. threw a leather bag over his frail frame, he yelled back assurances to PG, then closed the door.

"Dang, what was that about? It seemed like he had a new lead in his investigation."

"Really," Slick balked. "He earns a living saying those things. He was only stating the obvious. And I've been tryna find your father's killer for years." The deep sigh that left PG spoke of his disappointment and Slick didn't want to come off as insensitive. "But I do applaud what you're doing. I'm actually thinking 'bout throwing a block party in our old neighborhood to commemorate his death. But right now, we got more pressing issues on our hands."

"Like?" PG asked.

"Did you know they arrested 200?"

"They did, when?"

"Yesterday around six o'clock at Town East Mall. They shot a rubber bullet through his window, then snatched him out the car." Slick studied a pacing PG. "Did he pay you?"

PG looked off in thought. And in that brief second, he remembered the drunken night he spent arguing and sexing with Sabrina. Yesterday was 200's deadline to pay him by 12:00. Over six-hundred thousand dollars. Damn how could he forget? PG didn't have to answer the question, his body language did it for him.

"My point exactly. That's why I told you to stay focused on the task and let go of this wild goose hunt. We had one of the best and most respected plugs in the country in our good graces. But now he's breathing down my neck. How do you expect to pay him?"

"But I thought you paid him already." PG showed confusion.

Slick did, but this was PG's money that was owed. They didn't call him Slick for nothing. "Yeah. I started to until I realized that this wasn't my mishap, it was yours. And if you expect to keep things kosher on both ends, then I suggest you take care of it."

PG fixed his mouth to protest but Slick simply nodded and left the room. He began to marinate on Slick's words about paying the plug but brushed that off, because he knew he'd eventually do it. But what about 200? And Jaylen? He had planned to kill 200 anyway. But now that he might not be able to pay him, all his attention had turned to Jaylen.

Chapter 24

"Muthafucka!" Detective Winters flailed his arms so hard that his blue suit jacket seemed to float in the wind. He began to pace the crime scene, distraught and confused, the cold morning clouds a stark contrast from the heat rising off his head.

When a colleague approached to tell him, "The bodies had been here all night…" he brushed him off quickly.

"Not now."

He continued pacing for a full minute strong as if he was the only person on the clustered scene. Reality had set in and crumbled his vision. He had been building a case on 200 for over a year. And now his one trump card, Zilla, the person who could finger him for Buck and Mia's murders was sitting in a black body bag with enough wounds for twelve people.

He came to a halt as he massaged the razor bumps under his chin. "All this time… all this fuckin' time." He shook his head. Now it seemed that his investigation had reached a standstill. But he wasn't accepting defeat. No way in hell.

"Come here." Detective Winters waved over the young suit that approached earlier, who seemed ready at his beck and call.

"Sir…"

The detective's words were deliberate and barely hid his fervor.

"Corner off every end, from the neighbors' houses on down. I know 200 had a hand in this. And we're not leaving here until we find something."

"Well… we might have already found it," the suit studied Winters. "Because I just got a call that said 200's sitting in jail."

Chapter 25

The gray electronic door latched firmly behind 200 as he entered his assigned pod inside of Dallas County. The intake process only took seventeen dreadful hours, two taunts from officers that he could cancel going home, and two bites of food that he immediately regretted. But now amongst the curious eyes inside the noisy dayroom, he would finally get a chance to do what he'd desperately been yearning to do, use the phone.

Sitting his personal tote on the ground, 200 squinted about the congested area for the phones like he was looking for water in the middle of the desert. He found them not far from the TV, along the back wall. And much to his displeasure, they were all taken.

"Aye, fam, can I get next after you?" 200 asked a dude who looked at him crazy, making him feel the urge to clutch a pistol. Before 200 gave in to his impulse to go off in dude's shit, he unconsciously smacked his lips, then moved on to the next stool. "What about you, skool? Anybody call after you?" The stocky dude with the shag pointed back at two brutes standing in the middle of the dayroom, one of which seemed zeroed in on him.

"Yo, I got you," the last stool spoke up and saved the day. Then he did a double take and said his name with recognition. "200!" The guy deferred his attention back to his conversation. But it was clear he was ready to look out, which was good, cause 200 was damn near on the verge of taking off. He needed to get in contact with Jaylen like ASAP. And he felt like their bullshit conversation could wait. In fact, he was ready to end it for 'em. Did these niggas not know that his brother's life was on the line? He got caught up thinking about the dangers Jaylen might be facing since PG wasn't paid, when dude called out to him.

"200, here you go. You probably don't even know who I'm iz. But we cellies. We'll catch up." Studying him closer, he asked, "You good?"

"Yeah, I'm good," 200 lied when he really was going through it. He hadn't even grabbed the phone yet and already his heart was thumping. As he sat on the cold stool, the vibrations of his heart seemed to grow more frenzied. He just needed to hear Jaylen's voice and make sure that PG didn't live up to the threat of burying him first. He dialed Jaylen's number and got a surprising answer.

The number you called is no longer in service.

"Not in service?" He frowned. 200 dialed again, thinking this had to be some type of mistake. Less than three weeks ago, he'd bought Jaylen a new phone. *Now this bitch hollerin' not in service. Nah, that had to be wrong.* Intently, he listened as the operator processed the call. But after a few seconds, it said the same thing. He dialed again. And again, it said the same thing. He felt crazy being so relentless dialing the number, but this was just something that he couldn't accept. *The fuck was going on?*

After running into the same dead end, confusion plastered his face. It was hard for him to wrap his head around the fact that the phone wasn't in service. Especially when it seemed like just yesterday, he took it by Coach Phil's estate.

He was confined to that thought for so long that he didn't even realize that he had the phone dangling by his side until a demonstrative dude asked, "Aye you gon' use that?"

Yeah, to go across yo fat ass head with if you don't get the fuck up out my face, he thought. But he answered instead with a civil nod.

200 slid his body straight on the stool, then dialed a new number, this time calling Queen. He was hopeful to hear her assuring voice, one that could soothe his stresses and help him get much-needed answers. But after reaching her voicemail for five minutes straight, he only ended up getting fried out. Finally, he just said fuck it, and gave the phone a rest. It wasn't doing him no justice to just sit there clanking numbers.

200 moped back over to his tote, then paced the dayroom listlessly until the dude that was supposed to be his celly marched over. He was much taller than he noticed, sported tats on his bald head that spoke of his street ties, but he had a humility to his voice that softened his vibe.

"Say Two, what's up? You still don't remember me, do you? I'm Ju's big brutha. The one that went to the feds for hitting that armored truck."

Staring at him, 200 began to nod faintly. "It's coming to me." But his mind was too consumed with Jaylen to process anything else. "Say, how long you been in the dayroom?"

"Sheit, all morning."

"Have you seen them show anything on the news out of Highland Hills?"

"Mmm …" The guy thought. "I did, matter of fact. The Twinz. A nigga came through and put they fire out."

"That's it. Nothing else?" he asked, praying he didn't mention Jaylen. Each second that he took felt like an hour had passed.

"Come to think about it, I don't remember seeing anything else."

But thinking wasn't cuttin' it. It left room for doubt and 200 needed to learn something to still his restless heart. He grabbed his tote, then walked over to the TV and quickly engaged the dudes in front of it.

"Say, y'all watching this?"

They began to look amongst each other, but the consensus was neither here nor there.

"Hell, y'all mind if I turn it on the news?"

Nobody gave any protest and 200 changed the channel to CBS, which was showing today's forecast. Anxious and nervous, he gave it his undivided attention. He wasn't concerned with his warrant or his possible involvement in the Twinz' murders. He just needed to see that Jaylen wasn't in the top stories. He folded his arms and sighed deeply as he watched in anticipation.

***

200 had been sulking for three hours straight. Not for what he saw on the news. The local report didn't say anything about Jaylen. He was going hard on himself about being in this fucked-up position. Especially when the logical thing to do would have been for him to pay PG as soon as he touched. At least then he could have stopped the bloodshed in their murderous war. At least then he would have known that the money to ensure Jaylen's safety was safely in PG's hands.

But nah, he took what he thought would be a short detour, giving in to his thirst to get at the Twinz. Even when he remembered a voice say, "Don't go back there." A voice that was barely audible then but seemed magnified now. It had him stressing like Tyrese was in *Waist Deep*. But he shook back now and was ready to get some real answers.

200 left his cell then entered the relatively empty dayroom. The phone that he was ready to clash over earlier was vacant, and it seemed to be calling his name. He took the invitation and dialed Queen's number like he was being timed. And as his eyes perused the dayroom, he got an unexpected answer.

"Hello. Who's this?"

It was a relief to hear Queen's sweet voice.

"This me."

"*Me who?*"

"200, dang. You forgot my voice already?"

Queen laughed into the phone. "Nah. Neva that. I just didn't recognize the number. Where you calling from?"

"From jail," 200 admitted, causing Queen's voice to rise. "Jail!"

"Yeah, I know. I think me and you feel the same way."

"200," he heard Queen sigh into the phone. "What are you doing in jail?"

Contemplating all his troubles, 200 took a breath, then gave the safest response. "Awhile back, I posted bond on a gun charge. And now they got me hemmed up until they can smooth everything out."

"So, what does that mean?"

"It means that I'ma have to sit here until I go to court. Which may take a few weeks. Maybe even a few months. But everything gon be okay, trust me," he softly assured. He purposely omitted his more serious troubles. He wasn't trying to scare Queen off by bringing up the open homicide cases and the basketball numbers they'd try to give him if they ever got closed. He'd get with his lawyer and deal with that later. Right now, he was focused on one thing.

"Babe, look, I don't mean to curb your concerns. But I've been having problems getting in contact with Jaylen."

"Do you need me to call him?" She read his mind.

200 exhaled sharply. "Please. Let me give you his number real quick." Feeling like she'd situated herself, he asked,

"You ready?" After running it down to her, 200 tapped his foot impatiently as she clicked over and made the call. He was hoping it was just this jailhouse phone trippin'. But seconds later when she merged the call, the operator delivered the same troubling message.

The number you called is no longer in service.

"The bill isn't due for a week. That's why I'm not understanding this shit, fuck!"

Hearing a loud bang, Queen asked, "Are you okay?"

200 said in the most dramatic way, "No, I'm not. There's some shit going on with Jaylen that I really can't discuss on this phone. I mean I want to, but I can't." He thought of Jaylen's safety then eked out, "Can you please come down here?"

"Right now?"

Nah, they cut off visitation 'till the morning. But it's super urgent. Can you drop what you're doing and come down here then?"

"Sure, Jason, I'll be there. Oh, nah, hold up... wait. I forgot I owe these surcharges. And you know they gotta get paid."

"Surcharges! You mean to tell me that you owe surcharges?" These were driver-related fines that could result in jail time. And they were in the way of relaying this important message. "Damn, Queen. All that money you got and you out here playing games."

"I know... I know. I've just been so busy launching this hair care line that it honestly slipped my mind. But I'll get it taken care of. You better believe it."

"So, how long do you think it'll take?" He sat on pins and needles listening to her hum.

"Well, today's Friday. And I'll get to the license place first thing in the morning. And it may take a day to clear. So, I'm guessing three days."

"Three days!" 200 repeated incredulously, absorbing the prospect. Three days. He was already a day late on PG's deadline. He'd be signing Jaylen's life away if he waited three days. "Damn!" He shook his head. His desire to save face was looking more grim. But 200 didn't become this respected being complacent. He was a gangsta. And gangstas thought. His mind quickly processed solutions and alternatives. "Okay then, do that. But in the meantime, can you contact Jaylen on Instagram to make sure he's okay? Nah, better yet, go by Coach Phil's place."

"Where does he stay?"

"He got one of those new estates out in Hillside. All you gotta do is turn into the gates. Drive straight for two minutes, and you'll see an earth-tone-lookin' house at the end of the cul de sac. 223, that's the address. Can you remember all that? Do you follow me?"

"Yeah, I follow you. New estate… Hillside… end of the cul de sac."

"You have one minute," the operator intruded.

"Looks like the call is 'bout to end," Queen's tone saddened. "Are you gonna call back?"

200 sounded about as sad as her.

"Nah, I'ma go lay back on this bunk for a minute. I need to get my head straight. You just get on top of that for me. Love you, okay?" 200 didn't really wanna talk. Thinking about how he shoulda bucked the police to get that money to PG, and how dirty cops were probably divvying it up had him sick.

Chapter 26

Slick stirred atop his expensive sheets to fight off a recurring dream. Normally, his master bedroom would have him floating on cloud nine. But as he toed that thin line between sleep and consciousness, a kiss that was meant to soothe him brought back images he'd been trying to escape for over twenty years.

Summer '99

A swirl of night wind cooled Slick's perspiring skin as he sat with a foot hanging out a two-door coupe Deville. The 'Lac was the same color as the casual Armani shirt he wore, beige. And he had it whipped on the curb outside of their North Dallas stash house. Even in his twenties, Slick dressed differently with his own unique flair for style. While other hustlers were rockin' the trendiest urban threads, he tried to present himself as a boss. That's because in his mind he saw nothing less. Always had, and always would. It was just a matter of time before his money caught up.

Slick had barely christened the blunt he'd just rolled when loud music from the house signaled the exit of a barely dressed ghetto queen. "Yo, Peanut. Where he at?" Slick was referring to his younger half-brother. Earl G, the one who was turning twenty-five, and the one you could officially call the boss.

Peanut glanced back at the two-story home and could see the silhouette of a party from the light inside. "Oh, he's stumbling around in there somewhere. Probably politickin' 'bout some money. Probably entertaining a lil groupie. You know how he do." The door opened behind them. "Speaking of the devil."

Earl G emerged from the home as black as leather, handsomely groomed, sporting a sparkling white smile that could lift your mood. He was draped in a colorful short sleeve Coogi sweater, wore red Wallabees, and donned a quality gold chain with Golliday Boyz in prominent letters. Seeing his brother, Earl G beamed, "What up, Slick G?"

The added G signaled mystique within the Golliday circle. A G in your name meant that you were a part of the real bloodline. But Slick just preferred being called Slick. He didn't feel that his father's last name warranted that much precedent.

"Shit, I was just revving up to go to the club with you. But drunk as you is, we might have to cancel those plans."

"Nah. Watchu mean? Look at me. I'm good," Slick insisted. "I ain't drank nothing but a bottle of Henn' and that Japanese shit that Kesha brought. Then smoked that lil bit of weed we snuck back from Cali with the guys." He did his best to stand erect. "See, I'm good."

It was hard for Slick to see anything because he got caught in his feelings. The Kesha he mentioned was none other than his high school sweetheart. They shared many firsts, even endured a miscarriage. Now she was just content with being another one of Earl G's bitches. But coming runner up to Earl G wasn't new to Slick. He even experienced it with his dad when he died and left Earl G with all his money and the coveted connect.

"I know you good. I can tell," Slick lied. "But it's really no big deal. If we don't step out tonight, we'll tear the club up tomorrow. Besides," he reminded, "we got our people coming down from the Chi' to pick up that load in the morning. You know how they are about being on point. It wouldn't hurt if you got a little rest."

"Look at ju," Earl G slurred. "Always so serious. Always about a dolla, bro. Man, that money ain't goin' nowhere. It's my twenty-fifth birthday and we celebrating, dog. And you can start by passing that mufuckin weed."

That's how Slick knew Earl G was faded. For that dolla, he'd be on standby like an Uber driver waiting to deliver. All you had to do was tell him where and when. But he wasn't even taking a hundred and sixty thousand serious. As Slick took a final pull, Earl G seemed to forget the weed he asked for and walked off from the car.

"Where you going?" Slick asked.

"To take a leak. Calm down, playboy. I'll be right back." He slipped on some gravel before catching his footing. "It's okay… it's okay." He put his hands up.

Watching Earl G head to the alley, Slick sadly shook his head. To him, a crew's leader should always be on point. But maybe he could show that type of stealth when he got his own squad.

Slick curbed the thought with a smoke-filled tote, which brought a red glow to his side of the car's cabin. It also seemed to make all his worries fade away. Had him nodding to some Underground Kings. Taking deeper pulls. He even gave a goodbye hug to a girl he met earlier that day. Then the song changed, and that somehow triggered thoughts of Earl G's whereabouts. *Now where this nigga at?* He surveyed the landscape. His mental clock had said that he'd

153

been gone for ten minutes. But it didn't take that long to pee. Add to that, they were in a full-fledged war with these niggas from the East Dallas projects. Something was telling him to go check.

After shutting the car door, Slick moved swiftly through the damp grass along the side of the house. It was dark out, but considerably darker, given the shadow between their home and the laundromat adjacent to it. A few steps later, Slick found some reprieve as he reached the edge of the brick paved alley. With his head on a swivel, he looked under the light pole's weak glow, hoping to find Earl to usher him back to the party. He saw some unkempt yards. A few curious dogs. But the birthday boy was nowhere in sight.

"Earl," he called. "Man, where the fuck this nigga at?" He was growing a tad more nervous, a little more antsy. Searching harder, he walked about ten long yards before his all-black loafers came to a stop. "Earl!" He flailed his arms. "Got damn, Earl! You serious? What the fuck you doin' out here like this?' Earl was sprawled next to an industrial size trash can. Possibly drunk. Possibly sleep. But upon closer examination, he could have possibly been hurt.

Sensing danger, he slid a .40 cal from his slacks as he reached out to touch the body. But before he did, a beat-up station wagon gurgled to a stop at the end of the alley. The occupants had their windows down. And even though he could barely see inside, he could see their hard mugs. He probably wouldn't have noticed them if they drove off. But their elongated pause emitted trouble.

Slick surged forward with his pistol by his side, ready to let loose. He was gaining ground like a runner on the final stretch before the wagon built up enough momentum to finally pull off.

Slick back pedaled, thinking 'that was strange, before turning and rushing back to Earl G's aid. He timidly shook then gauged Earl G's muscular frame. There was no blood visible, and from the looks, he was still breathing. So, what was causing this particular state? He was convinced it was the liquor. But before he could make sure. He felt a shadow then recognized the troubling gurgle of the beat-up station wagon from the other end of the alley. Nervously, he turned over his shoulder and surprisingly, was met with the flash and ferocious bark of several different pistols.

B'ddd! B'ddd! Bop! Bop! B'ough!

"Oh shit!" he yelled, fumbling over Earl G and pulling him to safety behind the industrial trash can. The metal beast absorbed the bullets with sharp pelts and repetitive tinks. But he wasn't depending on the trash can to protect him. He had a little protection of his own. He aimed his gun around the trash can, while wisely keeping his head hidden, hoping to hit nothing but scalp and eyebrows.

BOOM! BOOM! BOOM!

The exchange sounded like a brief fireworks show before the gun sounds were replaced with screeching tires and a fleeing engine. The ruckus peaked before fading like smoke clears. But it took a few courage building breaths before he grew comfortable enough to glance around the trash can. Thankfully, the coast was clear. But much to his surprise, Earl G still hadn't budged.

"Earl... Earl." He shook him with desperation. He couldn't get his brother to move for nothing in the world. He searched up and down the dark destitute alley and was about to call for help, until he caught the gleam of some keys out the corner of his eye. A flash of all the kilos and money they'd just separated entered his mind. These were the same keys that were used to lock those safes, the same keys that were passed down from their father like a crown, the same keys that... damn. These were the same keys that made Earl G a multi-millionaire overnight.

From a reserve of hidden resentment, Slick began to feel that it would have made them both rich, had Earl G done like he would, and split that shit down the middle. But once again, Slick was the victim of his dad playing favorites. He was showing the streets that Earl was the son he claimed. The one he groomed for this. And he did so, all the way to the grave. But Slick had to check his emotions. There was no space for him to be thinking like this, especially with his brother in this unknown state. Slick reached out for the keys, so distracted by dangerous new thoughts that when Earl G gripped his wrist, it absolutely startled him.

"Oh shit!" Slick's eyes shot open, heart racing. It took a while to free his mind from that summer he almost relived. But once he began to process the luxe surroundings of his master bedroom, his breathing gradually steadied. He felt a hand glide inside his pjs.

"Don't worry. It's just me," Jariah assured. "You were groaning from that nightmare again. And I wanted to do something to help." The lust in her eyes told him exactly how so as she swept her fine hair behind her shoulder, then took a taste of his length.

Slick was like a daddy to Jariah. In fact, she was close to the same age as his daughter. Only difference was, she probably was more demanding of his riches. Not to mention, his possessions or anything else he held of value. But with a head game like hers, he felt she absolutely deserved it. Slick shook his head, grateful that he didn't get to the part of the dream that haunted him. Then he laid back on an assortment of pillows and enjoyed the warm feel of her spontaneous tongue.

Chapter 27

"That's it, 223, that is it!" Queen perked up as she parked in front of Coach Phil's estate. She couldn't even lie. 200 had described the house to a T, from where she could find it, right down to its earth tone paint. Queen made it her mission this Saturday morning to get on top of things for her bae. Not only did she satisfy her delinquent surcharges, but she was here now to check on Jaylen.

The whistling wind greeted Queen as she stepped out of her compact Lexus. "Whew!" She immediately bundled her cute red bubble coat. "200 had better be glad I love him." At the moment, she was lovin' this house, though. A mini mansion. Not bad for Jaylen's coach. She could feel a calm emanating from the door as she approached. But she hoped they weren't asleep, 'cause she was about to make her presence felt.

KNOCK! KNOCK! KNOCK!

Queen banged the large brass knocker, then put her hand on the hip of her skin-tight blue jeans as she waited for a response. She wasn't Jaylen's people or nothing, but for making her baby worry like this, he had some explaining to do. She stared at the lion's head peephole with expectant eyes just waiting for a shadow to fill it. She was confident someone heard her. But after a good wait the front door was all she saw.

Questioning if someone was home, Queen did a quick inventory of the property, noticing the black Ram 1500 in the driveway. It wasn't like the home was completely quiet. When she put her ear to the door, she heard the artificial laughter from a TV sitcom. Queen found the doorbell and decided to make her presence felt like that. And if someone caught feelings behind it, then so be it. She was only trying to check on Jaylen.

Watching the door, Queen was lowkey expecting some type of backlash. But after all those overzealous rings, she still got no response. This made her light-skinned face start to pout. No one was answering. And the wind was biting like a hawk. Queen was right on the verge of saying, "Fuck this." But before she accepted defeat, she thought of the urgency and desperation in 200's tone. Even though she couldn't see him, she could tell he was going through it. She knew how much he loved Jaylen. So, she tried to be a good trooper.

She slid her hands inside her coat as she walked around the house. The pool was covered and the terrace served as a segway to the home. She cut through the outdoor furnishings that led to the glass door. And once she peeked inside, she knew there was no one there.

Turning back towards the front, Queen's steps were hurried. But when she passed the Ram truck, she got an idea. She hustled to her car and snatched a piece of paper off a yellow memo pad. On it she scribbled, "Jaylen, this Queen. Please call me soon as you get this. Your brother's in jail. And he's worried sick about you."

After jotting her number, a good gust of wind curbed any pleasantries. She darted to the truck and placed the note under the windshield wiper like she was being timed. But unbeknownst to her, as she was leaving, a dangerous wind threatened to push the note away.

Chapter 28

200 meditated on some words he underlined in a book. "The opportunity to defeat an enemy would be provided by the enemy himself." He was reclined on his bunk, reading *The Art of War* by Sun Tzu as if he was a professional in his study. It was hard to tell from the outside, but inside, he was enduring a real-life crisis. Having to bottle the emotions from not knowing if his brother was dead or alive was likened to a kettle not whistling when it was steaming hot. It was stress at its worst form. And he took to reading his celly's books and listening to his war stories to occupy his mind.

It turned out that he did know Ju's big brother, Kel, after all. Dude was a fool at plotting major licks, specifically on armored trucks. And had they been in the world right now, 200 knew they'd be thick as thieves. But they weren't his reality roared forward like a growl from a lion. He was stuck in this small hellhole, while Jaylen was going through God knows what.

Unable to curb his frustrations, 200 snapped the book shut then hopped out the bunk and began to pace. *Fuck that book. Fuck all this tryna stay level-headed shit.* Here it's been three whole days, and he hadn't heard anything about Jaylen. Sure, he had Queen out there going to bat for him. But they weren't face-to-face where he could tell her how to salvage things with PG. She didn't know about the money that was owed. Or how dire the situation was. And he still didn't know if Jaylen was dead or alive. *Oh, and he better be alive,* 200 thought as dark thoughts took ahold of him. *Or I'ma get out this bitch and kill everything PG love.*

200 got caught up in his own world of gettin' at PG. It was so real to him that he could see his body jerking from each loud slug. He wanted to punish that nigga. Not just PG, but everybody that would show up to his funeral to mourn his death. He was so far gone, seized by the hold of his thoughts, that he didn't even know the C.O. was calling him until he began to rattle the bars.

"... Goodwin. Got damn. Are you deaf?"

200 turned around to see the large white officer.

"Get yourself together. You got a visit."

"A visit? Me?" 200's brows raised in shock. But when he regained his composure, he asked, "Did they say who it was from?" Over the weekend, he was contacted by Daley, his lawyer, who promptly told him that Detective Winters had planned to come ask him some questions. Daley also told 200 that his taking a year for the gun was a ploy to keep him in jail and advised him not to speak with the detectives without him present. This was right up 200's alley, because if it was up to him, he would skip this visit as a whole. In his mind, Detective Winters was one of the ones who curbed him from ensuring Jaylen's safety. And as frustrated as he was, 200 was liable to do something he'd regret.

The C.O. started to shake his head. "Does it matter who it's from? Just put some fuckin' clothes on and come on."

"Yeah, it matters," 200 countered. "With yo big dingy ass. Is it gon' kill you to answer a simple question?"

"Look, I'm not going to sit here and argue with you. You got about sixty seconds to get ready. Otherwise, I'm closing the door."

200 gave in to his curiosity and ran to hit his grill. But before he really got started, the C.O. yelled out, "Thirty seconds."

Damn nigga, he thought, brushing his teeth harder. He didn't even have time to argue. The C.O.'s accelerated count continued.

"...Five... four... three... two..."

As 200 rushed a towel over his face, he heard the door partially being closed. "Hold on...hold on!" He tried to catch the door.

***

Once 200 finally entered visitation, he shed the vibe of the guard that led him. This wasn't a visit from an attorney. Or one from a detective. Somebody had come through to fuck with the kid. 200 moved tentatively, glancing from the paper he was given to the numbers atop the cubicles, looking for 116. He took notice of the families who visited their loved ones behind glass. Most of them women and children. And they all seemed really joyful. 200 tensed in anticipation as he neared the gray aluminum dividers of his cubicle. Then as he peeked inside it, he was hit by the joy bug himself.

200 rushed to the stool and grabbed the phone. "Jaylen!" The sight of his handsome brother in a University of Texas jumpsuit had him more grateful than someone at sea being rescued.

"What up, brodie?" Jaylen responded.

"You, man ... You what's up," 200 beamed. As he took bro in, his mind drifted to how he'd been staking out the news every cycle. All the sleepless nights. Seeing Jaylen now was beyond fulfilling. "I see you got your hair dyed, lookin' all grown on me now. What the fuck's going on? Where have you been?"

"I've been at UT, attending some clinics about NILs. We did some seven-on-seven drills too. It was fun."

"So, what," 200 started, "you drive a few hours to Austin and that expensive ass phone don't work no more?"

"Actually, I lost it." Jaylen came right out and said it. "I mean, we looked and looked but it just never popped up. Now I'm waiting on Coach Phil to buy me a new one."

"You and these phones, Jaylen. Boy, I tell ya." 200 shook his head. "But I'm glad there's people like your coach around. Hope I finally get to meet him."

"Oh, he brought me up here. He's out there in the lobby. Said he wanna talk to you before we leave."

"That's a bet." 200 nodded. "But what's up with you, though? Man, you just don't know how happy I am to see you."

"Bro, I'm happy to see you too. I was so worried about you when I got Queen's letter. I wasn't tryna lose you to the system. We already lost Mom."

"Bruh, it ain't nothing to be worried 'bout. Nothing at all. Them hoes ain't got nothing on me. Just a bullshit gun charge." 200 went on to explain what that gun charge meant. He didn't sugarcoat about the year he was facing. He even prepared him to spend some more time at Coach Phil's. "They just tryna keep me in here, hoping they drum up something more serious. But they fishing in the wrong pond. I've been out the way."

They spent the next thirty minutes talking about football. Their mom. Being responsible. They even laughed their way to that hickey on Jaylen's neck.

"It's not what you think."

"Let you tell it," 200 countered. "Let me find out what y'all was 'really doing down at UT."

Jaylen blushed knowingly and 200 laughed. They were having such a good time that time just seemed to fly.

"Alright, I'ma need you to wrap it up, Goodwin," the guard's words intruded, sucking the air right out of the room, and seemingly 200's lungs. The thought of Jaylen leaving had him feeling like he might suffocate at any minute. But 200 did like he was programmed to do and hardened his heart to emotions. He was unsure about when he would see Jaylen again and wanted to make the most of this opportune time. He brought his fist to the glass.

"You know I love you, bro, to the fullest. I've been through hell and back tryna make shit shake for you. And no matter what situation I'm in, I'm always here for you."

"I love you too, bro." Jaylen brought his fist to his side of the glass, studying the earnest look in 200's eyes. Their fists met with a slight bump, but it was like they were forging something heavier. A rare bond. It was obvious this family was forever. 200 tried to ride a lil more, but suddenly, Jaylen hopped up from the stool. "Aye, let me give Coach Phil a few seconds before they end our visit."

Before 200 could protest, Jaylen rushed out the room, leaving 200 yearning to call him back. He thought about flagging the guard to get him to stop Jaylen, but then he ran the risk of the guard saying the visit was over. "Damn," 200 groaned. He wasn't ready for their time to end. It seemed like it'd just started. Plus, there was so much more to tell or warn him about. 200 didn't even get to alert Jaylen about the danger he was facing, or from who. But maybe he would do better explaining the situation to Coach Phil. He could break it down to him and advise him on how to move. He didn't have to tell Jaylen. This was grown folks' business.

As the room filled with the emptiness left by Jaylen's departure, 200 fell into a funk as he began to face his problems. The expired deadline. The fact that he was stuck in jail with no bond. The money that was owed in police custody. And the threat PG planned to enact if he didn't get it. The more 200's reality set in, the more he wanted to just break through these walls and get home.

As he stared at the ground trying to formulate a plan or solutions, a large shadow found the opposite side of the cubicle. Shortly after, a hauntingly familiar voice spoke into the phone.

"200."

This sent 200's mind on an instantaneous trip. For some odd reason, that distinct rasp had him going. He thought about a conversation he had with Coach Phil over the phone. One where Coach Phil was at Jaylen's banquet. He remembered it like it was yesterday.

"Coach Phil. Glad to hear you're finally back in town."

"Good to be back, too. I'm normally not away from home for that long. But I was at a realty conference. Business. You know how that be…"

Nah. What 200 knew was Coach Phil sounded familiar, and he swore he recognized that voice from somewhere. *But where?* In another milli second that 200 spent staring at the ground, his mind conjured more thoughts, one of PG in the living room of his home. Then a few of the threatening pictures of Jaylen he got on his phone. His head shot up.

No fuckin' way!

"PG! What the fuck are you doing here on the phone?" 200 exploded to his feet. "This was a visit with my brother. He was supposed to send in Coach Phil."

200's chest heaved from anger as his glare fell to PG's most noticeable features, his bushy beard and that distinct scar over his left eye. Looking to his hand, 200 noticed both of Jaylen's missing phones. Then PG had the nerve to sport that smug smile that 200 wished he could shoot right off his fuckin' face.

"You call me, PG. But the kids and staff at school call me, Coach Phil." He straightened the collar of his blue Duncanville polo. "Do I look the part?"

There was so much rage running through 200 that all he could do was laugh. *Phillip Golliday. PG. Coach Phil.* It all started to make sense. "Man, I knew I knew that fuckin' voice from somewhere," he said with conviction. "It was you all along. You were using my brother to get the drop on me and my moms' whereabouts."

"Nah, I was using your brother to get my money back. You know, the money you killed my siblings over. The money I gave you two weeks to give back."

"About the money... I can still pay you the—"

"Nope, that deal is dead. And until I decide if I want to shoot your brother in this lobby or punish him over time, consider him dead too."

"Wait. pick the phone up. We can work something out," 200 called desperately. "Bring yo muthafuckin' ass back here. You bet not do shit to my brother!"

Chapter 29

A middle-aged white sergeant, fresh on her evening post, halted her first drink of coffee mid-sip and rushed down the hallway. It seemed the closer she got to the jail's observation wing, the louder the violent kicks to the door became. It sounded like a raging bull was tryna leave the room.

"Are you alright?" she asked earnestly, looking through the glass at a shirtless 200 pace and brood. Word on the compound was that she could be a bitch. But if you caught her at the right time, she wasn't half-ass bad. 200 began to answer her back with expletives that were muzzled by the cell's thick walls, until she pointed at the intercom built into the metal door. Now she regretted she did.

"Hell nawl, I ain't alright," his magnified voice boomed. "They made a big scene out of nothing at my visit, first off. Now I'm stuck in this bitch and can't make a call when I got an emergency on my hands."

"So, why would they make a big scene at your visit?"

200 thought about all the hell he raised trying call PG back to the booth, the cursing, the confrontation with the laws. His eyes met the sergeant's. "I don't know. These

people could do the most sometimes. But that's neither here nor there. Can I please use the phone?" He tempered his tone.

She looked from the vomit on the toilet, to the pepper spray on his discarded shirt, and even the maniacal look in his eyes. Clearly, it was more to this story that meets the eye. "I'll have to go check."

"Go check?"

"Yeah." She stood her ground. "Usually when they put someone in here, it's for at least thirty days. And with all this ruckus you causing, it don't look like you going nowhere anytime soon."

"You think that's something?" 200 stormed back over to the door and got in kicking position. Boom! Boom! Boom! He kicked like a mule. "Get me to a muthafuckin' phone."

***

Feeling someone breathing on her neck, Sabrina looked back. "Jason Jr.! If you don't get your tail back in that car seat, it's gon be me and you," she chastised her adorable toddler. Jason Jr. brought his hands to his mouth to cover his mischievous grin, making Sabrina shake her head when he ignored her request. Fortunately for the Black and Mexican beauty, she was going through a car wash and the snail's pace they were moving at posed no real threat.

"Here, let me get that." She wet her thumb, then wiped a smudge of Cheeto crumbs off his cheek, before brushing more off his chest. "There you go, handsome." After Sabrina returned to watching soap coat the visible spaces of her Camaro, she felt Jason Jr.'s tiny hand stroking her flowing hair, something he did when he wanted something.

"Cut that up, Mommy," he asked excitedly.

Her fair skin scrunched. "What this?"

"Yeah… yeah... yeah!"

Sabrina cut the bass up to Black Youngsta's hit just to see what he would do.

"… That booty… Can I touch that booty… Can I play on the booty," he jumbled the words, making Sabrina buss out laughing.

"Un-uh. You don't need to be worried 'bout touching nobody's booty. If your daddy hear that, he gon beat your lil behind."

"Where's Daddy, Mama?" His dimples flared with joy. "Can I see him, huh? Is he still out of town?"

Still out of town? His question bounced around her head. *Where did he get that from?* Out of town.

Sabrina nodded passively, still wondering what he was talking about, out of town. Then it dawned on her that she'd been using that lie to cover 200's absence. Call it what you want, but it sounded better than telling a toddler that she wasn't fuckin' with his dad. Or that his father cared more about his brother than he did his own son. But that was before she learned the truth in 200's heartfelt voicemail. A lot has changed since then, including the man who brought her out of that dark time, PG.

As the death of his close siblings set in, Sabrina attributed PG's mood swings to that. But then being distant, uncaring, and aggressive became a habit. And that was something that she couldn't go for. It all spiraled to a head when PG got a room at the Omni and insisted that she have a drink with him. 'Come on, ma. We on our five-star shit. A lil pink Rose won't hurt."

She politely told him that she didn't drink during her pregnancies. And he came outta nowhere, talkin' 'bout, "I'd bet you'd do it for 200." Huh? What? Did this nigga really … From there it went all the way up.

PG accused Sabrina of being in contact with 200. And she yelled about who was he to talk, when she hadn't been by his estate in almost a month. "Why the fuck are we renting a room when you got a million-dollar home, Phillip Golliday? Is there something up there you don't want me to see? Somebody? Another bitch!" PG responded by palming her face and smushing her backwards. She caught an Uber home that night. He'd been in her doghouse ever since.

But like time had a magical way of healing all wounds, it put a pretty lil Band-Aid over hers too. Sabrina couldn't honestly say that she was mad at him right now. Maybe she could order up some takeout and invite him over to talk.

Sabrina felt breathing on her neck again. "Mommy… Mommy! Ooh look, it's soaping the car back up," he pointed at the blue foam.

"Yeah, I see it." she turned to meet his grin. "Hold up. Wait. How did you get my phone?" With the quickness, she snatched it from his wavering hand. That's when she noticed that Jr. had accidentally dialed PG's Facetime. Boy, what have you done? Seeing PG in his place of business and oblivious to the recording underway, she was about to close the app. But then she heard PG spill a familiar name. One that made her tense.

"Yeah, 200 knows now that I'm the coach Jaylen's been staying with. The cat is officially out the bag. You should have seen his face, though, when I popped up at the jail. Homey looked like he'd seen a ghost," PG boasted.

"The boogeyman," someone off camera laughed.

"The muthafuckin' Grim Reaper or some shit like that. Yeah, brodie had the dick look on his face, fo' real. But it's only gon get worse when he sees what happens to Jaylen next."

"Ooh look, Mama," Jr. was trying to say before he was swooped up and shooshed into the car seat in one motherly motion. Sabrina put her phone on mute shortly after. And chimed back into their conversation as fast as her heart was now beating.

"PG, you said that like you got a trick up ya sleeve. What exactly is it you plan to do?"

"Well…" PG rubbed his hands, "I don't want to give it all away. But just know that the fate Jaylen's 'bout to suffer will make national headline news."

169

A chair squeaked and a clap ensued as the two shook hands. Sabrina recognized now that it was his boy, Whitey. "Boy, you sho'nuff is crazy. I mean crazy, fo'real. But I'm finna dip and go make this play. What you 'bout to do?"

"'Bout to head over to the palace and kick back with something exclusive—"

"Who, 'Brina?"

"Nah," PG's comment made her gasp. "Baby mama been on some bullshit. So, I had to go get me a fresh rotation."

Different emotions seemed to swirl inside Sabrina's heart like a flock of birds. She closed the app, but was so far gone that she didn't even feel the phone slip from her hand. PG had told it all. Everything she'd been wondering and more. Yes, he was cheating. And it was no doubt now if he killed poor Renee, because he had Jaylen at his home planning to kill him too. These revelations had Sabrina telling herself, "I'm Not Gon Cry" like Mary J. Blige. And looking back on things, she knew she couldn't. Renee was murdered because she told PG who was the suspect in his siblings' ambush.

And as the emergence of blue skies signaled that her car wash had ended, she felt indebted to keep the same thing from happening to Jaylen.

Chapter 30

"There must be some type of mistake," Queen told the DPS worker as she looked from her bathroom mirror to the gray phone atop the sink. Queen waited sufficient time to see if her surcharges had cleared. So, she didn't understand why there was a problem going on. Queen felt a bit of assurance when she heard the DPS worker typing. *Yeah, get it together*, she thought, before an encouraged voice echoed through the speaker phone of her Galaxy.

"You did say Huddley, right?"

"No, ma'am. I said Hunt...ley. Queen Huntley. H.u.n.t.l.e.y."

Queen noticed, herself, how she stressed the pronunciation of Huntley. Maybe because she had a respect for it that she wanted the worker to mirror. That surname was special because it belonged to her deceased mother. A name Queen later changed hers to when she was old enough to drive. It made her feel that special connection that her mother always brought her, and was a declaration that her shortened legacy would continue to live through her. Besides, even though they were in town, she barely knew her father's side of the family. From what she heard, they were nothing to play with. And her father was the worst one.

"Hmm..." the DPS worker uttered, foreshadowing a response. "Okay. My apologies, Ms. Huntley. I didn't hear your name clearly. And it *is* showing in my computer that your surcharges are satisfied and currently clear."

"Well, that's good news. I bet my boyfriend gon love that. You have a good one, ma'am. I'ma get back to getting ready."

Queen used an expensive nail to press end on her phone, then finished styling her crinkly hair, using her own brand of products. She was in a rush to be early for an important meeting. "Because being on time meant that you were actually late," she recited from a business book. And that was something this girl was most definitely about, her business. She became a viral sensation with the funny way she advertised her afro-centric hair care products. Catching the attention of scores of consumers, as well as some regional retailers. Now, the big dawgs were calling.

Today, she was scheduled to meet with national retail giant, Target, about a game-changing vending opportunity. The prospect was so exciting that she adjusted her pink terrycloth robe and began to practice how the meeting might go in the mirror.

"Thank you, Tandra, for the introduction..." Tandra was Queen's brand manager. She's the one who's been behind the scenes, putting everything in motion. "As you can see from our charts, Organic Gro is a great way to target an audience who want to see a reflection of themselves when they walk in your stores. Oh, you think so as well. And you want to buy the whole inventory. Well please make out a check to Queen, LLC." She put on a faux show of smiles and waves but stopped her silliness when she heard the phone ring.

Looking every bit like the Dallas version of Nu-Nu, Queen crossed a white throw rug, then leaned over the his and her sink to check the screen. Seeing the strange number, she initially squinted. But then her angel face softened when she realized it was 200. She greeted him by singing the chorus to Jazmine Sullivan's "Need You Bad." And her light rendition made a light crack through 200's heart of stone.

"Dang, girl. I don't know what it is about you, but you always put me in a good mood. I be needing that shit. 'Specially with the way I've been goin' through it."

"Long day?"

"Man, if you only knew. But I don't know why I even said that. Just forget I brought it up." 200 tried to change the subject. But Queen wasn't hearing it. She didn't understand why he insisted that she talk to him about anything but was reluctant to do the same. She used his line that, 'We in this.' And after a little pouting, her persistence finally won out. 200 told Queen that Jaylen came to visit. That he spazzed out and went to seg right after and would've been stuck there, had he not convinced the sergeant to let him make it. He told her it was more to the story than meets the eye. But what he told Queen next made flutters fill her stomach.

"That's why I need you to come visit me. So, I can lace you up about Jaylen. There's certain shit we just can't say over this phone."

"Today?" Queen asked, already thinking about her important meeting.

"Yeah, today. But you gotta check in by 4:00, cause visitation closes an hour later."

Queen took the phone away from her ear and saw that it was 2:45. If she went down there to visit him, then she could kiss her meeting with Target goodbye. "But, bae—"

"No buts, Queen. This is important. That's why I've been stressing how urgent it was. It's a matter of life or death." 200 felt some trepidation coming from Queen's end and reiterated somberly, "Life or Death."

"Okay," Queen said, without realizing she did.

"Thank goodness!" 200 clapped. "Go 'head and get ready. I'll see you in a few."

Queen leaned against the sink in front of one of her products, then sighed as her shoulders fell, and dialed her brand manager's number. "Hey Tan," she started. "About that meeting…"

***

At a quarter to four, Queen entered the Dallas county jail still partly distracted by what could've been of her meeting with Target. Hopefully, the excuse she gave Tandra was enough for them to reschedule. She had her doubts they would. But what's done is done. She cleared her throat as she slid her license in front of the desk sergeant.

"I'm here to see Jason Goodwin," she announced, only to find the officer in a trance. Queen had put on some black Givenchy printed jeans that propped her curves like she had a bbl, wore shiny heels to show off her toes, and her Tiffany & Co. necklace sat atop her cleavage like a treasure. Seeing the guard shake his head, she felt a little rewarded. She just hoped she got the same admiration when 200 saw her.

"You gotta excuse me. It's rare that we see girls as beautiful as you," the large white officer shot his spill. But he was out of his league. "Now where was I?"

"Jason Goodwin."

"Oh, yeah. Jason Goodwin," he remembered. "Let's log that in and get you that visit."

Hearing him enter her credentials, Queen glanced around the lobby and back to the desk where her mind started to drift. She genuinely hoped Jaylen was okay. For Jaylen's sake. For everybody's. She just wondered how the situation could be dire if they just had a visit. She knew niggas in jail would say anything to remedy their stresses. And with all she had going on, she hoped this wasn't the case.

A sudden head jerk from the officer made her musing fade and after he shook his head a few times she was all ears.

"You're gonna have to come back Saturday and get that visit. 'Cause it looks like somebody already beat you to the punch."

"I'm sorry, come again?" Queen's brows shot up. But what she really wanted to ask is, "What the fuck did you just say?"

"I know. It threw me too. And I even went back to double check it. And it's showing that Mr. Goodwin is currently at visit."

"At visit how? At visit with who? I mean, we just got off the phone. You can't be serious?"

"I'm afraid that I am," the officer said like he empathized for her. But he was really taking pride in dropping salt in 200's game. If it wasn't for the last visit where they had to wrestle 200 to the ground, he wouldn't have a sprained shoulder and be subject to desk duty. Sure, nobody asked him to escalate the situation, but he couldn't stand what 200 represented. And he wanted to sneak a beating in on him while he had a chance. "Look, you seem like you don't believe me. And I can get into a lot of trouble for this. But I'll even show you. See?" He turned the screen.

Seeing the name Sabrina under Jason's made Queen's heart skip a beat before it came buffering back, filled with heartache and pain. She never expected 200 to make her feel this way. It was a feeling so foreign that she didn't even know how to react. This wasn't like her 200. The 200 she knew made her feel protected and understood her better than any man she'd ever known. That's why she would do things, like risk her own well-being and welcome 200 in her home. Or up and say fuck a meeting of a lifetime just to be by his side. It was because they were supposed to be "in this." But judging from the name on the screen, and the excuse about Jaylen that he probably told to Sabrina, it's apparent they're not.

Queen grabbed her license off the counter and said, "I'm done," then tried to make it out to the car before her tears came tumbling down.

***

"Why didn't you bring my son?" 200 quizzed rather coldly as he studied Sabrina's reaction from his side of the cubicle. He felt like after he apologized, she should have been got at him. So, there was no point in fronting like shit was just gravy.

Sabrina adjusted the phone, then raked a strand of hair behind her ear, her mind too cluttered to catch his attitude. "I think he knew I was coming. He usually gets excited when he sees the babysitter. But he cried the whole time to go with me. You're all he talks about."

"Well…" 200 looked at her like she was dumb. "Why you ain't bring 'em?"

"'Cause there's something that I need to talk to you about."

200 absorbed the seriousness in her eyes, then dry laughed. "What, that you're pregnant? 'Cause that's none of my business. That's between you and that simp ass nigga that knocked you up."

"No, it kinda is."

"Kinda is what?"

"Your business. It's the baby's father that I need to talk to you about." Sabrina took a deep breath and looked at the polished ground, before looking back through the thick security glass at his curious gaze. Knowing how much he loved Jaylen was making this harder. But the only way to help the situation was to flat-out tell him. "I've been seeing this dude since we stopped talking five months ago. And the other day, I overheard him tell one of his runners that you knew he had Jaylen. He said your name specifically. But what made it even worse was that he said his plan to make Jaylen suffer will make national headline news."

Alarms rang in 200's head. "Bitch, you seeing PG? The nigga I'm beefin' with? That's who you pregnant by?"

Sabrina felt the heat coming from 200's words like a radiator. She didn't know whether to run or hide. "I-I didn't know."

"Bitch, you knew," 200 countered. "So, save that shit for somebody else. I can't believe yo stupid ass. Went and had a baby by the fuckin' opp." 200 shook his head as he fumed just staring at her. The mere sight of his baby mama had him disgusted in the worst way. "So, what he do, Sabrina? Did he break your heart like you thought I did? Now you over here telling me, hoping I'll ex him out? But what's gon happen when you think I fucked up again? You gon run back over to him and keep pitting us against each other?"

"Jason..." Sabrina looked at him with hurt in her eyes. "It's nothing like that. I was just tryna warn you about Jaylen."

"Bitch, don't tell me what's it's like. 'Cause I know you, Sabrina, know you like the back of my muthafuckin' hand. You get emotional and fuck shit up. But you better know this..." He aimed the phone at her. "If something happens to Jaylen or my Junior, I'm holding you personally responsible."

Sabrina cowered in fear as he slammed the phone down and left the room. This was definitely a side of 200 that she didn't know.

Chapter 31

"You called me?" Jaylen stuck his head inside PG's palatial home office. PG waved Jaylen inside but continued to talk through his phone's headset. He sounded professional as he gave off assurances. But unbeknownst to Jaylen, he was putting the order in for his demise.

"Thank you. That won't be an issue," PG told his Cali steppa. "I have someone very important here. I'll get back to you soon." After taking his headset off, he greeted, "Jaylen is everything alright?"

"If this is another check-up about my mom, then yeah, I'm doing fine."

"Actually, it wasn't," he dryly laughed. "I was simply checking on you. But since you brought her up, I got something that'll make her proud." PG motioned for him to have a seat at the imported cherrywood table, then spun his laptop to face him. "Take a look at this."

Jaylen saw the image of what appeared to be a large private school. He hunched his shoulders. "Okay, what am I looking at?"

"Possibly the key to your NFL dreams," PG formed a crooked smile. "If you're ready to get out of your comfort zone and step up to the plate." PG came around his side of the table and absorbed the image with Jaylen. He started nodding his head as he let it marinate. "This here is Botsco Prep, the richest school in California, and the number one football team in all of America. Like us, they play a national schedule with games spotlighted on ESPN. But get this, their players are allowed to sign Nils."

"Nils?" Jaylen asked in shock.

"Yep. Nils. California pioneered a bill which permits their high school athletes to earn money off their name, image, and likeness. And Adidas wants to take advantage of it and spotlight you. They want to pay you a hundred thousand dollars to star in a commercial. But this is just the tip of the iceberg. By the time it's said and done, you can very well be the richest prep star ever."

Jaylen tried to play it cool, but his brown skin did little to mask his excitement. He pinched the peach fuzz under his chin. "So, how will it work?"

"You'll have to move to San Bernardino—"

"Wait a minute," Jaylen paused him. "And leave Texas?"

"Of course. That's if you want to participate in the Nils, that is." PG pivoted back behind the table to his padded chair and relaxed his hands behind his head before continuing. "But the school has prearranged for your half-a-million-dollar tuition, with room and board, to be paid by their wealthy trust. And they have the highest quality facilities and offer the best education.

"But what about my brother?" Jaylen asked earnestly. "He's all I got."

PG seemed empathetic to his statement. But he really didn't give two fucks about his brother. In fact, he was doing everything in his power to bring him to his knees. The entire motive for Jaylen coming to Cali was so he could whack him out west and make it harder for the authorities to track the murder back to him. He seemed hell bent on punishing 200 for his siblings' murders and cleaning out his stash house for one and a quarter mil.

"Now, Jaylen," he continued his deceit. "I hate to be the bearer of bad news. But your brother's in way more trouble than he led on. There's a possibility he could get charged with murder and never come home. And with the spotlight that you've created, you don't need that type of trouble around. You've got to learn, like other people with great success, that everybody's not meant to get on the elevator with you. I get that you have a special bond, and it will always be there. But this Botsco thing is a gamechanger. And it will give you the platform your talent deserves. Just sleep on it," PG said as he started out the room. "You're considered the Lebron James of football. Why not brand yourself like it?"

PG didn't press any further because he felt he didn't have to. What teenager could turn down the chance to be rich before they were old enough to drive?

Chapter 32

A bottle of alcohol exploded against the wall, sending shards of glass all over the bedroom. "Bitch, if I ever find out you told someone about my secret, I'll kill you myself. You hear me?"

These words echoed in Queen's head before the winter wind picked up, bringing her back from her childhood to her mother's gravesite. Queen proceeded to shake off any lingering remnants of that recollection, then did what she came here for, and placed some purple tulips atop her mother's headstone. Like clockwork, on her birthday, Queen would visit her mother's gravesite. To reflect. To talk. Or to just flat-out think. Mostly about what really happened that fateful day her dad pulled her out of school. And considering how much her parents argued, her mother's passing felt a little suspicious. At this point, she was desperate for closure so she could either quit harboring this ill-advised blame for her father. Or dead her relationship with her dad completely.

She blew a kiss goodbye to the heart-shaped picture engraved in the headstone. But right as she turned to leave, her phone began to vibrate like crazy. It was three long rings before she was able to fish it out of her tan Chanel clutch.

But when she saw it was 200 calling, dejection covered her angelic face.

Queen sighed from her nose as she thought about hitting the famous "fuck you" button. She was the type of girl that if she was done with a nigga, she didn't let him back in. But being with 200 made her do things that she couldn't explain. And despite their recent troubles, a part of her yearned for his comfort. Before her self-concept got the best of her, she hit accept. But she didn't fully open herself back up. She just held the phone to her ear.

"Hello... Hello," 200 said with urgency. "Queen, are you there?"

But Queen just kept walking the pristine green grounds towards her Lexus.

"If you are, it would be nice if yo pretty ass said something. I haven't heard from you in like three days, since you was 'sposed to come visit. I hope you not in your feelings 'bout that. 'Cause I'm already in mine. My baby mama dry popped up and ruined my chance to see you. Not to mention that conversation I've been tryna have with you about Jaylen. Remember what I stressed. It's a matter of life or—"

Queen abruptly hung up. "...Death."

***

200 punched one of the dayroom phones back on the receiver.

"Damn, big homie," a sweating Kel peeped him. "You alright?"

"Man, I've been tryna reach Queen's ass for three days straight. And the day she finally answers, she don't say shit. What the fuck!"

Kel knew his celly was going through a thang right now and tried to help him curb it. "Well, take it out on that flo'. Next set of push-ups on you."

200 balked at the idea, scanning Kel's circle of workout disciples. "Fuck a push-up." He would much rather take it out on a niggas' shit. All a nigga had to do was look at him wrong, or act like they wanted smoke. But since nobody bit the bullet, he fell in line and got some paper. For now.

As 200 fired off one adrenaline filled push-up after another, evoking excitement from the crowd, something he read filled his mind. "The opportunity to defeat an enemy will be provided by the enemy himself." He couldn't explain why this popped in his head. He knew he wasn't losing his mind. But, while he was on the subject of enemies, he definitely had one on his radar. This nigga PG was going to pay for bringing him stress like this. He may have had the upper hand right now. But before it's all said and done, PG was going to bleed. And that was on Renee!

Struggling with the last few push-ups, he finally tapped out.

"Damn, that was eighty-two." Kel patted his shoulder. "You barely even work out. That's good as fuck."

200 didn't pay the praise much mind as he caught his breath like a sprinter. His mind was too clogged with trying to figure out what he could do to ensure Jaylen's safety. Even when somebody he knew from the streets tried to show him something on the news, he seemed in his own world. But he still heard him.

"Look at this nigga." his darky pudgy finger pointed at the TV. "In line to be chief, when back in the gap, he used to be a whole street nigga. He 'posed to had took PG and his siblings in after they father got killed. I just think it's mighty funny that he blew up right after that."

Hearing PG's name, 200 broke his neck to look at the screen. And when he saw someone that he was related to, his blood instantly boiled.

"Well... well... well... Look at the Gollidays. Back at it again," uttered the boisterous dude who shunned 200 over the phone before, as he stepped too close to 200 for comfort.

Mugging him, 200 felt thirsty for blood, like a pitbull who had finally broken free from his chain. Then he felt Kel pat him on the shoulder.

"Tight, it's back on you."

But his fist unconsciously clenched.

***

"C'mon, Two… You trippin', dog." 200's thoughts went back forty-five minutes as he sat with his prominent lawyer inside the jail's attorney-conference room. They were addressing 200's concerns. An opportunity 200 was fortunate to have. Because if it wasn't for his celly, it would have been an opportunity missed.

When Kel followed 200's mug and saw the way his fist clenched, he pushed him back to their cell before 200 ended up crashing out. There, he told him straight up, "Fuck all this frustration shit. You need to think about how you can help your situation now." Their pact to hit armored trucks together could have been Kel's motive. But it still helped, nonetheless.

200 shook the devil off his back long enough to think about the money he'd stashed in the Aston. Six hundred fifty thousand that the police never claimed, that they probably never found. And as he prodded his lawyer, in between other questions, to gauge what he knew, he felt a sense of hope that the money was still there. And he could use it to save Jaylen.

"So, they can just release it to you like that?" 200 asked about his towed car.

"Maybe not like that," Daley clarified. "But barring any detainers, we should get your precious Aston back to you soon."

"Sooner rather than later." 200 gave a feeble smile. "Can't let these tow fees rack up." But he was really desperate to see if the money was there.

As Daley uttered a response, he suddenly paused, looking around as the power in the room flickered on and off. It seemed to pass without incident, readying Daley to placate 200, before it completely clunked out, making it pitch black and drying up all the A/C in the room.

"What the fuck?" surprisingly came from 200's lawyer, as well as a chorus of gasps and frustration groans from surrounding rooms. You could hear the backup generator as it tried to kick in. But it was an unpleasant twenty seconds before the power was restored.

Guards rushed in the room shortly after. "Mr. Daley. You're gonna have to resume your visit another time. I assume you know the protocol. We have to do a special count." The guards rushed Daley along like he was the president, and they were the Secret Service. But it didn't stop Daley from yelling over his shoulder before he left the room.

"I'll have my paralegal to get on top of that. Just be patient, will ya? Don't worry about a thing."

Not worrying was going to be easier said than done. It practically started when Daley left and 200 realized he didn't get to ask about a new bond. As he shook his head and began to toil in thought, it didn't take ten full seconds for the door to come open again. Only this time, it was trouble.

"Mr. Goodwin," Detective Winters greeted in a deep rasp. He was accompanied by a pair of peckerwood detectives who had an air about them like they'd been in the Army. They seemed to look at 200 with disdain, while Detective Winters reached for a handshake as if they were actually cordial.

200 stared at him like he was crazy. "What the fuck is that on yo hand?"

Detective Winters followed 200's eyes to the black streak on his palm then slowly pulled it back. "Oh yeah, that. That's grime. I must have got it when I cut the power to the breaker off. It's a lil trick we used at the county. Cut the power, and it takes about twenty minutes for the cameras to reboot. It gives us a little time to do some convincing, if you know what I mean? But, of course, you do," he boasted, leaning on the table. "The whole county knows how we play a little foul. But enough about that. You look good. Nice to finally catch up."

200's face screwed as he thought, *nice to catch up, my ass*. He wasn't a fan of the detective's threat or that fake ass smile and wasted no time chopping it down. "Well, I wish I could say the same about you, but you look like shit. Dem razor bumps on yo neck look like the before picture on a shaving commercial. You smell like a carton of cancer sticks. And since they booted you off *The First 48*, you look all bummy and dry."

"Ha-hah. Real cute, son. But that should be the least of your worries. You should be more concerned about names like Taj, Heavy, Buck, and Mia." Detective Winters noticed a flash of suspicion in 200's eyes. "Ring a bell?"

"Might sound familiar to my lawyer. Matter of fact, why don't you check with him and see what he has to say?"

"Or why don't you stop being such a hard ass," fumed a frowning peckerwood. "Before we take advantage of these cameras being off and make good on our reputation."

200 had a bunch of fly shit to say right on the tip of his tongue. But it was best that he did what he did and laughed and looked off. Getting into a war of words with them would make them think they had action. And he wanted to make it clear, he didn't have shit to say. As he fell into a shell, ignoring their hostility and anger, he nodded calmly as if he was in a complete state of bliss. He ignored their theories of why it happened. He caught himself when they mentioned his mom. But when the taller peckerwood slammed his billy club into the table, it was like poking a bear.

"Hey you, listen, dammit," he grilled 200. "We're not here to play games. Now if you wanna play dumb, then you could look dumb. Right in intensive care for the next two weeks."

"Well, do it!" 200 sprung to his feet and flipped the table, causing a great big commotion. "If y'all can put this nigga here in intensive care, then you gon' have to make me know it." Just the threat of not being able to help Jaylen had him seein' red. And if they got in between that opportunity, he was ready to go all out.

Detective Winters saw the way his chest heaved and the fire in his eyes. "Just what I thought. The temper of a killer. We'll see how much you're huffing and puffing when you're staring down this life sentence."

A light wind rose from the door as they closed it, and when 200 found himself alone, he wanted to grab his hair and scream. There was so much going on in his head that he didn't know what to do. His cases. Looming cases. Death... death... and more death. And he still hadn't figured out how he was going to save Jaylen.

He started pacing like Cuba Gooding Jr. in *Boyz N Da Hood*. But before he imploded and yes, it was a struggle, he cleared his throat and desperately sought a reprieve. "Lord, you know that in spite of my ways, I still pray. And it's crazy, but man, there's so much weight on me right now, that if a piece of lint fell on my head I might fall to my knees. I just need you to clear my mind of this unrest until I can save Jaylen. Until we can save Jaylen. Can you do that?" He thought about Jaylen. "Can you do that for me, please?"

Chapter 33

About 2,500 miles away in Atlanta, amidst ideal gray afternoon clouds, Tasha hopped out of an Uber at a Zone 6 paint shop. Tasha was a new face in town. But from the way she ran the city, you would have thought she'd spent five years here instead of five days. She shopped at Midtown boutiques, laughed it up at cultured salons, even consulted a digital marketer from her leased loft at the Twelve. The digital marketer showed Tasha how he could boost her following to eighty thousand. And she couldn't wait to model on the 'Gram and carry out her plan to get this *guala*.

As she maneuvered through some expensive toys you might find on *MTV Cribs*, she looked ahead and saw the stocky well-groomed paint shop owner awaiting her arrival. She noticed him shaking his head as he studied her body. And she bet it had something to do with the way her goods were stuffed in the shorts of her tan Gucci jumpsuit. It was a mild seventy-two degrees, a stark contrast from the winter weather in the 'D, and she felt it would be a good time to break it out. She also felt it would be a good time to rock it with no panties. Being a bad girl was now a part of her official persona.

The owner greeted Tasha with a clap and a warm smile. "Glad you could make it. I see you lookin' stylish as usual. Come on over, so I could show you how 404 Customs do." He led her a few feet away to an embroidered tarp that covered her painted Lam' truck and grabbed it at the bottom as he prepared to snatch it off. He looked into her nervous eyes. "You ready?" he teased. When Tasha nodded profusely, he told her, "Okay, feast your eyes on this."

"Oh wow!" Tasha's eyes lit up at the flawless, sky-blue paint job. She clapped her hands with childish glee. "Ooh, me like."

"Me like too," he said, taking in her body. But the chocolate hottie was way too excited to notice.

She walked around the truck. "You even painted the lips on the rims sky-blue. I can't even lie… you got this lit as fuck."

Tasha knew that 200 told her to take the Eurus to get chopped. But she figured if she just got it painted, she would be alright. She didn't know that having this truck was like having a pistol with a body count. And if a detective did some homework, it could connect them to the St. Louis murders.

"And just so you know," the owner started, "I decided to waive your twelve-thousand-dollar-fee. I just wanna show you that if you fuck with a nigga like me, I'll spoil you a lil different."

Tasha could tell from the earnest look in his eyes that he wasn't trying to stunt. It made her gush at his generosity. "Aww, thank you." She gave him a hug, then agreed to stop by his Bankhead club for "one drink," then waltzed back over to the Eurus. "Can you do something for me?"

"What?" he asked.

She went through the settings on her phone. "Snap a picture?"

He wanted to see what she was about to do. "Yeah… fa'sho."

Opening the door, Tasha started to twirl her finger in her sky-blue streaked ponytail. "And if you really good at it, I might let you take some mo'." She led him on with a sexual slug. She hiked a Gucci designed Chuck Taylor on the frame of the open door, then looked down to make sure that soft round ass was properly tooted. Dude told her the pose was boss. A title she fell in love with in St. Louis. And if her treatment since she stepped in that role was any indication, she was about to hit IG and turn the fuck up. Playfully, she placed a small hand on her ample butt cheek. "Should I hold it like this?" And dude smiled, then took the picture.

"Perfect."

Chapter 34

200 stared listlessly through the security glass at visitation, fighting grogginess from a restless night of sleep. It was 8:00 am and he didn't expect to get a visit. But when he saw Queen's silhouette, his whole demeanor changed. "Got damn, look at babe. Lookin' all good for her nigga." He blushed, seeing her familiar face. It was like her eyes had a different glow and all his stress went away. Though that changed in a hurry when he saw Queen having friction. The way the cubicle was set up, he couldn't see who was causing it, or even hear for that matter. The security glass was no joke. But the watch on their thick wrist let him know it was a nigga. A nigga who was about to get himself killed.

Before 200 knocked on the glass, Queen diffused the situation. But he didn't fully slide back until she grabbed the phone and took a seat. "Who was that?" he asked with concern and confusion on his face.

Queen looked over her shoulder before answering. "Trust me, you don't wanna know."

"I don't?" 200 took exception. "I don't know how you figure that when I'm like two seconds away from coming through this bitch and getting on a nigga's ass."

191

"Hold on… hold on. I didn't mean to say it like that. It's really not that big of a deal. So don't read too much into it."

"So, that argument I just seen you having, the one where your arms were flailing. That's not that big of a deal?" He detected something different in her angel eyes.

"Nope," she broke eye contact. "We weren't even arguing."

"You sure?" he asked.

"Positive. It was really nothing at all."

"Well, if you say it was nothing it was nothing," 200 finally let it go. "I'm just glad your pretty ass here. What's been going on?" Before Queen could answer, 200 continued as if he didn't ask her a question. His excitement to see her took over and he started venting a hundred miles per hour. He admitted how he'd been doin' the most, trippin', letting his frustrations get the best of him. Getting out his body on just about whoever and how it almost cost him. Then he clarified his legal woes, the gun charge and why they revoked his bond. But he left out the part about Winter's investigation. He wasn't tryna scare baby off.

"And then, Jaylen… Damn, Jaylen, I don't even know where to start with that." But seeing her staring off with her arms folded, he decided to start over. "My bad. I been so busy tryna bring up Jaylen that I didn't even stop to see what's going on with you. You aight?" Queen ignored him, which had him wondering what's wrong. "What… you mad or something? I'm tryna read you, but you won't look up at me… Did I do something wrong?"

"I don't know. Did you?" Queen raised a brow.

"Not that I know of."

She was disappointed that he didn't already know and sighed roughly into the phone's receiver. "Typical."

"What does that 'posed to mean?"

Queen unfolded her arms and glared at him with fire in her eyes. He wasn't sure he wanted to see what happened if she let it loose.

"It means don't have me breaking my neck to come see you. Only to get up here and find out you cakin' with yo baby mama—"

"I wasn't cakin' with my baby mama, let's be clear on that. She just popped up out the blue. I thought she was bringing my son."

"Did she bring him?" Her foot tapped as chatter from the other cubicle filled the silence.

"Huh?"

She was tempted to say, "If you can huh, you can hear." But she felt so played by the ordeal, she didn't even bother.

"Look, Queen. I'm tryna tell you it's not what you think—"

"I don't know what to think," she cut him off. "All I know is what you told me. You told me to come up here because you had an urgent situation with Jaylen. 'Baby, it's important. It's a matter of life or death,'" she mimicked his masculine voice. "Do you know, by coming up here, I missed out on a chance to get my products in Target? Then, I didn't even get to see you. Do you know how hard I worked for that?" After a brief pause, she smacked her lips. "You know what, fuck that. I only came to help with Jaylen. Just get to that part." She folded her arms.

"Dang, you didn't come to see me?"

Queen didn't hesitate to answer.

"Nope."

"Not even a little. Like this much?" He gestured with his hand.

Seeing his smile, Queen had to implore some resolve to fight off one of her own. She wanted to let him know she wasn't feeling this situation, so she kept her face serious.

"Nah, it's only 'cause I love you and I look at Jaylen like family that I even came up here."

200 studied her glossed lips. "You look good saying you love me."

"Shut up." She blushed. "I didn't even mean to say that. You get on my nerves, Jason Goodwin. Now tell me what's going on with Jaylen."

"Well first, lemme tell you I apologize that you missed your meeting. I know how important that is to you. And I want those opportunities for you. And rest assured that me and my baby mama ain't got nothin' going on. She was actually here to bring up Jaylen. Or rather warn me about his coach. And I'ma get to that. But first I gotta know, is me and you good?"

After she spent a second trying to block her true emotions, her voice broke with a solemn softness. "We good."

"Cause I'm grateful for ya. And I don't want you thinkin' for one second that I don't know what I got." 200's eyes floated over her soft black ensemble. "And I'm damn sure grateful you rockin' that Dior for me." Before he could add how he was surprised that they let her in with that on, a shadow emerged behind her on the wall. Followed by a man wearing the wristwatch that he noticed before.

Queen followed the malice in 200's eyes and gasped at the man's sight. Then she tried to clean it up with a smile. "Excuse me. I'll be right back." After a few steps, she gave 200 another polite smile, then grabbed the man by the arm and pushed him out of sight. Any other time 200 would have noticed the way her perfect booty moved so loosely. But pussy was the last thing on his mind. If this nigga got out of line, then it was up.

200 stewed from the incident before his emotions gradually settled. Then he tried to wrap his mind around where he'd seen dude before. Not just his watch— *him*. He was certain he'd seen him somewhere. He had a certain mystique about him that you just couldn't ignore.

As 200 racked his brain for a few minutes tryna figure it out, Queen snatched the phone from the hook, dispelling his thoughts. Her fair skin was now flushed red and her posture screamed she was in her feelings. It was hard to tell if she even wanted to talk.

"That dude, that's the one I seen you arguin' with earlier, right?"

Queen blew some hair from her face before she finally sat forward.

"That's not some dude. That's my dad. And he's pissed that I came up here. Telling me no daughter of his is gonna visit a man in jail. That's what all that was about earlier. He literally tried to stop me. But who is he to tell me who I can and can't love?

"Hold up, wait," 200 pictured his face. "So, that's your dad?"

"Yep."

"The one you think did that, you know, to your mom?"

"You mean, the one I think killed her. Yeah, that's him. He thinks he can run me like he ran her. He gets on my nerves. Uggh!"

As Queen opened up to him like she was in a confessional, 200's mind began to mull a million miles a minute. He thought about her mom's secret. A conversation he had in the day room. The pictures of her parents on the nightstand. Ain't that a bitch.

"What are you smiling about?"

"Nothing. Just something I read in a book. It said: *The opportunity to defeat an enemy will be provided by the enemy himself.*"

"Huh? Where that come from?"

"Don't pay it no mind. I need you to do something important. Come over here real quick."

200 rushed to the corner of the security glass and waved Queen over. Here they could talk without their conversation being recorded.

"Can you hear me?" His voice echoed like he was in a empty room.

"Yeah."

"Well make sure you listen close, 'cause I need you to be on point. As soon as you get to the car, I need you to call my lawyer and tell him you're the person I'm having him to release the Aston to. You remember that bag you gave me?"

"The one with the money?"

"Yeah. I think the police never found it. And soon as they release the Aston, I want you to go in the stash spot and check. Once you get that understood, have Daley to call up here cause I need him to do something that's urgent for me … Fo'real. Do that. Tell him it's super urgent! He might come with an excuse like he in a meeting or some shit. But don't let him off the line until you get him to call."

"Wait," 200 was taking her too fast. "What's going on?"

"You said you wanted to help with Jaylen. Well, here's your chance."

Chapter 35

PG was chillin' in his lavish kitchen with a real-life Barbie when the buzzing of his smartphone hardened his facial expression.

"Scuse me." PG got up then walked over to the marble counter. He wasn't feelin' how the caller threw a monkey wrench in his game. So, whoever this was calling, it had better be for something important. He snatched the phone then silenced the alert. But upon seeing a strange number, he was tempted to slide the phone in his designer slacks. All day they'd been hittin' him with random quotes and frivolous questions. But curiosity got the best of him, and he opened the text.

"How fuckin' cute!" he seethed.

"What?" He ignored the concerned blonde.

It was a picture of his son, Craig, as he arrived home from school that had him clutching his phone with an unusually tight grip. The frail teen was alone, and didn't even know he was being recorded. But what tripped PG out was, how this number even got it? That question was answered seconds later with another vibrating text. Which almost immediately made a snide smile form under PG's thick beard.

"As you can see, I can get 2 you are your family at any time. Try anything fly and the boy dies."

The screen quickly lit up again.

"Instructions will be given for Jaylen's safe return. I suggest that you keep ya eyes peeled for that."

Although PG was mad enough now to hurl his phone against the wall, he was able to cool himself down to the point where his mind could reason. It was obvious to PG that 200 was behind the text because ironically, holding his nuts, he used his own words against him. And now, come to think about it, he scratched his smooth waves. The previous text he skimmed over might not have been that random at all.

Taking a closer look, PG swiped down the touch screen with such haste that he had to center it a few times just to read the old messages. One said, "Fair exchange ain't no robbery. And the other one asked was his power back on after it briefly went out at his home. *He knew*! PG thought. That son of a bitch knew. He was just dropping a slug about the power to show that we could be touched.

To PG, this was reminiscent of the 200 that niggas gossiped 'bout. Rapped about. He even heard of 200's prowess from his own squad. But far as PG knew, 200 was sitting in a cell. And if he's still sitting in a cell, *could he really reach out and touch me*? The answer made PG gulp from nervousness. But he quickly steeled his resolve with a nice swig from a bottle of Rémy. The liter hit the counter with a slight thud. Then unexpectedly, he felt a soft hand glide inside his blue button-down shirt.

"Is there something I can do to help?" She pressed her perky breasts against his back. But PG was still rigid and barely acknowledged her presence. "What about that one thing you like when I do?" She smirked, running her nails across his chest. "C'mon, it'll be fun."

She grabbed PG's hand, then led him to a nearby stool with mischief dancing in her gorgeous green eyes. He could tell by her anxiousness that she was ready to act bad. But with the threat of a war imminent, sex was the furthest thing from his mind. PG was so far gone that he didn't even feel her hands as they slid up his thighs. Neither did he hear the loudness of her unzipping him. Or how she seductively said that she was gonna make it all better.

But he did feel the heat of her wet tongue.

PG looked down to see her skillfully holding him in her mouth as she used her hands to push strands of hair behind her ears. She was doing what she loved to do most, at least for him. And after a few seconds of suction, she stroked him a few times then admired her handiwork.

"See?"

* * *

Sabrina drove her Camaro deep into PG's gated community before killing the lights in front of his peaceful estate. As she stared at the front door, a surge of nerves washed over her. Things had gone from bad to worse for the expecting couple, and her showing up unannounced probably wouldn't help. For the past few days, Sabrina had been sulking about PG's devious secrets. And in their short conversations, she didn't let on what she knew. She claimed she had curbed that to try to focus on her plan to rescue Jaylen. But dealing with Sabrina and her emotions, it was hard to tell.

A button near Sabrina's rearview brought light to the car's interior as she did a once-over of her 90's themed earrings and airbrushed shirt. The Black and Mexican beauty was still as bad as ever, and felt that pregnant or not, she could seduce PG and sneak Jaylen from his clutches.

As Sabrina studied the mirror and refreshed her red lipstick, she noticed the emergence of light from the estate's front door. "I know the fuck this ain't," she started to say before her feet hit the pavement and she was outside the car. She began to charge towards the long walkway, her lovely sway quickening as some perky-breasted white girl waved goodbye to the person behind the door. The blonde was trying to get home before her husband arrived from a business trip but slowed her steps and waved naively to a surging Sabrina.

"Hi," she sung.

"Bitch!"

"Oh my God, please don't beat me up." She scurried across the lawn back to her pompous estate.

Sabrina charged about two more steps before taking off towards the house, where someone ducked their head back inside and magically closed the door. *Ohh, the nerve of this black ass nigga*, she thought, balling her fist. It was one thing to have to learn about his cheating through FaceTime. But to catch him in the act was a whole notha story.

Sabrina rushed to the door, then twisted the knob like an intruder. "Open this mufucka up. I know you seen me." She continued to twist the knob and was about to beat the door down, when she felt the breeze from the door being yanked open.

"Girl, what the fuck is you doing out here trippin' like this?" PG scolded.

"I'm trippin'? You standing here smelling like that bimbo's perfume and I'm the one who's trippin'? Move," Sabrina swatted him back inside the home, then slammed the door hard enough to shift the expensive artwork on the wall.

"Look, don't be slamming my doe like that."

"Fuck yo doe. What do you have to say about this bitch leaving yo home!"

"Bitch, I said don't be slamming my doe," PG gripped her jaw with unexpected force.

"Nigga, let me go. Let me the fuck go."

Sabrina didn't know that PG was dealing with the pressure of 200's threat. And seeing how she infringed on his hiding Jaylen, she may have pulled up to the wrong place at the wrong time.

"I guess calling ahead would have been too much for yo extra ass. But you gon learn about popping up at my shit like this." Snatching her by her Pocahontas-length braid, PG pulled her kicking and screaming all the way upstairs to his master bedroom, before one of the boys could see her. "Now sit yo ass down." He tossed her over a gold trimmed ottoman, which made her look up from the carpet with shock and fear.

"You've changed," she said solemnly, feeling hurt as tears misted in her eyes. "There was a time when you wouldn't even raise your voice at me. Now you handling me like this while I'm pregnant." She cradled her stomach.

"A lot's changed. That's life, so just deal with the shit," PG said coldly. "I wasn't complaining when I walked in that suburban home I got you and saw ya phone laid out with a text from 200."

He tried to walk off, but she grabbed his slacks and jolted to her feet.

"Really?" She batted his shoulder. "You're gonna drag me around the house like this while I'm pregnant. Then excuse it by bringing up some fuckin' text I never sent. Wow!" she said dumbfounded as shock filled her broken heart. This had to be how someone on *Maury's* show felt when they didn't recognize the person they once knew. "And to think, I was expecting you to apologize for this bimbo. Or maybe show some concern like a real man and come check on the baby. But no-h, you bring this up. Out of all the things." She shook her head.

"Sheit. For all I know, that could be 200's baby."

"Fuck you. I ain't been with nobody but yo no good ass." She hit him again. "While you standing there acting like you somebody's saint."

"Yeah, whateva."

"Whateva my ass. 'Mister, I had to go get me a fresh rotation.'" She folded her arms. "Yeah, I know that this ain't your first time cheating. And I also know the *real* reason why you've been keeping me away from here."

"Yo, Sabrina. What the fuck are you talkin' 'bout, real reason?"

"Don't look like that. You know exactly what I'm talking about...I gotta kick back with somethin' exclusive... baby mama been on some bullshit. Sound familiar?" She studied him with confidence before strutting into his circumference. "Your FaceTime. I stumbled across the whole conversation. And I already know that you plan to kill Jaylen. And you killed that boy's mom too, didn't you?"

PG smacked Sabrina to the floor hard enough to make Ike Turner cringe, then pounced atop her like a lion attacking a gazelle. "So, what if I killed his mom?" He roughly clutched her collar. "If I remember correctly, you was the one who told me 200 killed Buck and Mia."

Sabrina spoke through the ringing in her head. "No, I told you what the police thought. You didn't have to kill poor Renee. She was innocent in all this."

"So, you switching sides, huh? That's how you rockin'? This might explain why you was texting that nigga in the first place. Matter of fact," PG thought back to 200's last text. "200 said to be on the lookout for some instructions. Bitch, you came to bring 'em?" He raised his fist.

Sabrina's eyes bucked at the threat of another blow. "Instructions! What instructions?" she asked sincerely. She was coming to save Jaylen on her own accord. So, she was green to any instructions.

"Bitch, you know what's going on." He hauled off and swung at her face. But she ducked and balled up until he started to choke her.

"Aww! Stop. PG, please. You got too much weight on the baby. Boy, get up. You're hurting me!"

PG finally landed a blow which knocked her out cold. And when she came to, she felt a throbbing in her jaw and heard the barking of his words.

"Bitch, I don't give a damn about you or that baby." He stood over her. "Y'all can jump off a bridge for all I care." He flinched like he was about to punch her again. "Oh, I can't stand a traitor. I'm 'bout to go and take a leak. I suggest that you don't be here when I get back."

When the bathroom door slammed behind him, Sabrina rubbed her jaw. She pushed a wisdom tooth around before spitting it out. Seeing the blood on the carpet, she started to cry. It seemed like just minutes ago, she set out with good intentions. Now she was sitting here on this stain-proof carpet, battered and bruised. Nervously, she found herself pressing 119 into her phone. She looked at the screen and hastily corrected the blunder. It felt weird even calling the police. But she took a deep breath, then pressed a 9 then a 1.

***

Jaylen thumped the brochure he read about Botsco Prep as he paced around his room. "Cali, here I come!" He smiled. He remembered Coach Phil's advice. "Everybody can't get on the elevator with you." And as he saw himself embracing the hype of his own Adidas ad, it became easier to brace himself for any backlash from 200.

Jaylen left out the door to go and tell Coach Phil the good news. Coach might have had some company, judging from the noise he heard earlier. But Jaylen was sure he'd want to hear this. He walked past the stairs that overlooked the great room and went further into the east wing of the home. A few guest rooms later, he came upon Coach Phil's master suite. There was light coming from a small crack in the door. But as he began to announce himself, he heard a toxic argument that made him step out of view and put his ear to the door.

"Yeah, I know that this ain't your first time cheating. And I also know the real reason why you've been keeping me away from here."

Whoever this sassy lady was, she was giving Coach Phil the business. He wanted to give them privacy and started to walk away. But the next words he couldn't help but hear stopped him in his tracks.

"...Your FaceTime... I stumbled across the whole conversation. And I already know that you plan to kill Jaylen. And you killed that boy's mom too, didn't you?"

"Me?" Jaylen pointed to his chest, becoming a little bit saddened. He then heard what sounded like a hand hitting a turkey before he heard Coach Phil's unexpected response.

"So what if I killed his mom? If I remember correctly, you was the one who told me 200 killed Buck and Mia."

Jaylen went from listening at the door to falling against the wall. He knew he wasn't supposed to be in this compromising position. But it was like he couldn't will himself to move. Grief seemed to spiral from one corner of his body to the next. And once his reality set in, he started crying on the spot. How could his coach... the man who guided him on his college decision, who was seemingly there when nobody else was, kill his own mom?

That question lingered in his head as he staggered back down the hall and bounced off the walls and the rails until he made it back to his room. The warm heat and light music brought him a familiar comfort. But once he sat on the bed, he started to shake his head. How could he find comfort here? This was the house of an enemy. A man who killed his mom to get back at 200 and had every intention on killing him too.

Jaylen rose off the bed and paced the room as he fought to make sense of it all. During this confusing task, he thought he heard more arguing. And the grief that he felt was suddenly replaced by anger. He wanted to do something. It was a position that was foreign to his young mind. But he felt a natural urge to get at his coach. But how so?

That question was answered seconds later with an image of Lil Craig accidentally shooting a hole in the wall and the gun that he stole from his dad to do it. If Jaylen remembered correctly, Lil Craig hid it in his room. And before he knew it, he was out the door, storming in that direction. Jaylen came upon Craig's room about as fast as he scored a touchdown, then took the liberty of listening outside the door as he waited to twist the knob. From the flow of water, it sounded like Lil Craig was taking a shower. And he crept inside to hear him humming R&B behind the steaming bathroom door.

Jaylen rushed over to the large mahogany dresser and began to scrounge through clothes and personal things on his mad dash to find the pistol. He went from one part of the dresser to the next without much luck, before thinking about the dresser drawer and pulling it out.

"Bingo!"

Jaylen's eyes bulged, seeing the sparkling pearl handle .38 Special. The exact same one Lil Craig was in the living room playing with and showing off. Quickly, he grabbed it then like a seasoned intruder, put everything back in place before taking off out the room and back down the hall. From the pep in his step, you knew he was on a mission. But as he recognized the gun in his hand, he took an abrupt detour and went back to his room.

Closing the door, Jaylen took a deep breath. *Think about all of your hopes and dreams. Are you really go throw it away like this in the spare of the moment?* The inner voice felt like Renee was talking to him. Growing up, Jaylen had always been obedient to his mom. But the fact that she was gone and never coming back, he couldn't let that make it.

This time Jaylen burst out the door down to Coach Phil's room, passing the great room again, before coming upon his cracked door. Looking inside, all he saw was an empty room. Then he heard Coach Phil arguing with his guest about what she was doing with her phone.

"Bitch, I know you ain't called the police." Coach Phil stood over her, with his back to the door. He didn't even know Jaylen had entered the room.

"Mm-mm," Jaylen cleared his throat, never taking his eyes off him.

"Jaylen!" Coach Phil turned in surprise. Then he began to grow a little concerned by the way Jaylen was holding his hands behind his back. "Is everything alright?" He craned his neck.

Jaylen studied Coach Phil for a second, before whipping the pistol in front of him and aiming it dead at his chest. "You killed my mom?" Jaylen steamed.

"Now, Jaylen," Coach Phil stepped forward with his hands up. It was then that Jaylen noticed his brother's baby mama, Sabrina, on the floor.

"Sit." Jaylen pointed next to her.

Coach Phil laughed in contempt. "Just put the weapon down. It's clear that you got the wrong idea." He took another step forward, forcing Jaylen to step back and steady his weapon.

"I'm warning you. I'm not playing. And I'm not gon say it again. "Sit down," Jaylen stressed, putting on his hardest face. But Coach Phil continued to close the gap, making Jaylen mash the trigger.

Click! Click! Seconds later, Jaylen opened his eyes to see a defeated-looking Sabrina and a smiling Coach Phil.

 Click!

He went for broke.

"I took all the bullets out a couple days ago after I saw the hole y'all left behind the wall. Didn't want the wrong person accidentally getting shot, you know?" Anger filled Coach Phil's face as he walked up on Jaylen, then viciously smacked him to the ground then pulled out a pistol of his own. "Say hello to your mother for me. Your brother will be joining you soon." He cocked the hammer on a chrome fo'fifth back, then leveled it at Jaylen's head like the pro that he was.

Jaylen didn't even get to pray before he heard a deafening blast.

F'ough!

Followed by another one.

F'ough!

But he didn't feel any pain rushing through him. Slowly, he brought his shivering hands down to find blood in the middle of Coach Phil's forehead, and seeping through the chest of his blue button-down shirt.

"Freeze! Police! Drop your weapon!" a roar rose, followed by the influx of several officers. Moments later, Coach Phil's dead weight fell at Jaylen's feet. The officers rushed to their aid.

"Are you okay, ma'am... sir?" Jaylen was still shocked from witnessing the horrible tragedy and didn't even know how to respond. A black officer kneeled beside Jaylen and put an assuring hand on his shoulder. "It's alright. We saw him about to shoot you. And we had no choice but to put him down."

Fifteen Minutes Later

A fellow officer was the first to spot Slick as he raced to the crime scene and slowed his determined steps before he approached the home.

"Now, sir. I can't lie. It's a gruesome scene. I just want to warn you before you stumble across something you're not ready to see."

Slick swiped the new boot's hands from his black peacoat, then walked through a sea of police lights to the body bag at the foot of the lawn. "Open it," Slick instructed a plain clothes detective, his breath fogging against the cold of the night. The detective wrestled with the zipper before looking up at Slick and opening the body bag to PG's bloodstained beard.

"Oh, God... my nephew!" Slick covered his mouth. His emotions were like a bomb going into the air, it took a second before going off. Slick began to mumble incoherently as he walked in a tear-filled daze, his mind struggling to process what his eyes were seeing. These officers were used to seeing traumatic reactions from grieving loved ones. But rarely did they see this from one of their own. One officer reached out to console Slick, but he unknowingly stepped out of reach. "Y'all gotta excuse me." Slick shook his head. "This is a bit much."

Slick took a few listless steps before catching himself, then headed for the solitude of his tan unmarked car. Once inside, he took a handkerchief and wiped his crocodile tears. Then after slyly checking his surroundings, he pulled out a phone and dialed a trusted contact inside Dallas County Jail.

"Tell 'em it's done," Slick said, referring to 200's request.

"Will do," a deep voice assured before ending the call.

Slick didn't think that in a million years he'd be siding with the enemy. But after 200 had Slick summoned for a meeting, everything changed. 200 told Slick he knew the secret Queen's mom was hanging over his head. And if he didn't kill PG and safely return Jaylen, his whole world would change. Slick balked at first, viewing 200 as just some young punk. What did he know about a Golliday, other than his nephews had the bricks? But then 200 brought up skeletons that Slick thought he was taking to the grave. Pointing out how Slick killed Queen's mother to keep her from telling anyone that he killed his own brother. "How would Queen feel about this?" 200 asked. "What about yo nephew? What would this mean for your career, since you in line to be chief?" By night's end, 200 had Slick's corrupt crew on the hunt for PG. The opportunity just so happened to fall in their hands when Sabrina called the police.

Slick pulled out a cigarette, a habit he formed since PG hired the private investigator. If PG was to ever find out that Slick killed his father, Slick knew they'd eventually clash. "Sorry, Nephew. It's just a part of this dirty game," he said. Slick brought his square to a cherry as his mind replayed what happened that eventful day of Earl G's death back in '99.

***

Slick was reaching over his incapacitated brother for the keys to the safe when Earl G grabbed his wrist, making him gasp.

"Damn, Earl, you scared the shit out of me. You aight?" Slick's heart raced as he fought to mask his mischievous intentions.

"Yo, where I'm at? What's going on?" Earl G looked around groggily as he sat up on his elbows in the dark alley behind his home.

"You don't remember? Fo 'real, dog?" Slick raised a brow. "I came out here to check on you after you came to take a leak. Next thing I know, niggas was hanging out a station wagon dumpin' on our ass."

"Nah, I don't remember none of that. I really don't." Earl G massaged his head. "All I know is, I was partying having a good time and I ended up out here," Earl G said in a weak rasp. As he complained that his head hurt and continued to gather his wits, Slick's eyes swept the perimeter as shady thoughts filled his mind. Slick knew that behind every rich man was an even more sinister crime. And as he remembered the commas that were tucked away in the safe, he sensed an opportunity to commit his.

"Is the party still going on? Did you hear me, bro?" Earl G searched Slick for a response. But Slick responded by upping a '40 and firing violent shots through his chest and chin.

P'ough! P'ough!

Slick was wrestling to put the pistol away when a couple members of their crew came bursting through the alley.

"Where the hell y'all been? My bro's been hit." Slick *pretended to resuscitate him. "The shootas took off in a beat-up station wagon." He pointed towards the end of the alley. Seeing them follow the treadmarks, Slick reached beyond Earl G and grabbed the flickering safe keys and put them in his pocket.*

As the sirens on an ambulance blared before its exit, it brought Slick back to the present and the chaotic scene outside of PG's estate. It was almost impressive to him that 200 orchestrated this. He had to give it to the young boy, his mind turned out to be his sharpest tool. Sitting idly as flashes of light bounced off his face, Slick didn't want to go back to the house and relive his deadly transgressions. "Fuck it. I'll just tell them I was grieving," he said to himself. He started the unmarked car and drove off.

Chapter 36

Queen fanned herself with a handful of big faces as she sat behind the glass at visitation across from 200.

"You got it?" he asked, perking up in anticipation.

"Yeah." Queen could barely contain her excitement.

"Dang, that's crazy. I kinda sensed that it might be there. But after they had it for so long, I'm surprised that it was." 200 was referring to the six-hundred fifty racks that he stashed in the Aston. The money he got jammed up with before he could get it to PG. But with PG in a nice coffin and Jaylen tucked away at Aunt Doonie's, the money was his to spend how he saw fit. "Aye yo, look," he spoke assertively. "I want you to take two hunnid of that to Aunt Doonie. Tell her to find a nice home in the suburbs to move her and Jaylen. Not in Texas though. Go somewhere like Florida or Michigan. But get my brother as far away from this nonsense as she can."

"You look content." She took notice. "It seems like doing this for Jaylen puts you at ease."

200 thought about what he set out to do for his family. "I guess you can say that. But I'm not done. Get with my lawyer and tell him I said pull the rabbit out the bag." Seeing confusion on her face, he added, "He'll know what to do." This was code to get Slick to come to the jail. *Yeah, bring ya slick ass up here. We got shit to do*, 200 thought.

Getting Detective Winters to drop the murder investigations was number-one on that list. Then he was gonna have his future father-in-law to get him probation on the pistol. And with the chief in his pocket, there's no telling what he could do.

"And since you've been loyal and trustworthy," 200 continued, take a hunnid of that to help grow your business."

"Fo' real?" she gushed.

"Yeah, and keep the Aston too. I gotta put a stamp on yo pretty ass and let the streets know that you're mine."

Queen stood in her heavenly get-up.

"Boy, you bedda be lucky this glass right here. Otherwise, I'd be all over you." She studied him with lust.

"Well, since you can't, just blow a kiss right here for now." He pointed at his tatted neck.

"What about there instead?" She looked at the pants of his county jumpsuit.

"Sheit, you can do that too."

"Muah... muah... muah." Queen blew playful kisses.

Epilogue

Eight Years Later

Jaylen took the Dallas Cowboys hat and put it over his short, dyed dreads, then shook the NFL's commissioner's hand with unexpected vigor. He had just been drafted with the fourth pick by his hometown team. And he stood with a confident posture as his handsome face beamed. Cameras from across the packed arena continued to flash and his smile was so big his jaws could barely contain it. Finally, the commissioner gave Jaylen an authentic white and blue jersey. And he flipped it front to back and said, "How 'bout dem Cowboys!"

A courteous usher came over and directed Jaylen across the stage to a homely blonde reporter who appraised his strong frame with a beaming smile.

"Jaylen Goodwin. How does it feel to say you're officially in the NFL?" She tilted the ESPN mic and placed a hand on the shoulder of his Miami-themed suit.

213

"It feels amazing, honestly. There's no better word to describe it."

"And I bet it feels even more amazing that you're playing for your hometown team?"

"No doubt, Jill. It's like a dream come true. I couldn't have scripted it any better. One minute, I was adding myself to the Cowboys roster on Madden. Now I'm tryna help bring a title back to the city," he said, evoking cheers.

"Now this dream of yours wasn't always a fairytale," her clear voice sobered. "You had a rougher road than some of the other draftees. How difficult was it for you to get to this point?"

Entertaining the question, Jaylen let out a sigh that reverberated in the microphone. "I'm just fortunate." He shook his head. "Fortunate that I was able to overcome ..." He tried to remain strong by looking off from the camera and breathing back his tears. But the memories her question brought up were a little too much. A small yelp escaped him, making the jam-packed arena feel his pain. Even the reporter had to lift her glasses to wipe away tears. But if he learned one thing from his challenges, it was to continue to fight. And he took a small breath and tried to steady his speech.

"With the help of my beautiful mom, Renee, I persevered. She was killed when I was a teenager. But it was like my brother said, she was always right here." He patted his heart. "I love you, Mom! Thanks to you and Jason for helping me get here. We did it, y'all!" He smiled through his tears. "Cowboys, here I come!" He waved goodbye.

Lock Down Publications and Ca$h Presents
Assisted Publishing Packages

Due to an increase in the price of services we have increased our prices. The prices below reflect the price increase as of 11/1/24.

BASIC PACKAGE	UPGRADED PACKAGE
$699	**$1000**
Editing	Typing
Cover Design	Editing
Formatting	Cover Design
	Formatting
	Upload eBooks to Amazon
	Upload Paperback to Amazon
ADVANCE PACKAGE	**LDP SUPREME PACKAGE**
$1,400	**$1,700**
Typing	Typing
Editing (line editing/content)	Editing (line editing/content)
Cover Design	Cover Design
Formatting	Formatting
Copyright Registration	Copyright Registration
Proofreading	Proofreading
Upload eBooks to Amazon	Set up Amazon Account
Upload Paperback to Amazon	Upload eBooks to Amazon
	Upload Paperback to Amazon
	Advertise on LDP's Amazon and Facebook Page

***Other services available upon request.

215

Additional charges may apply

Lock Down Publications
P.O. Box 944
Stockbridge, GA 30281-9998
Phone: 470 303-9761
Email: lockdownpublications@gmail.com

Submission Guideline

Submit the first three chapters of your completed manuscript to ldpsubmissions@gmail.com. In the subject line add **Your Book's Title**. The manuscript must be in a Word Doc file and sent as an attachment. Document should be in Times New Roman, double spaced, and in size 12 font. Also, provide your synopsis and full contact information. If sending multiple submissions, they must each be in a separate email.

Have a story but no way to send it electronically? You can still submit to LDP/Ca$h Presents. Send in the first three chapters, written or typed, of your completed manuscript to:

LDP: Submissions Dept
P.O. Box 944
Stockbridge, GA 30281-9998

DO NOT send original manuscript. Must be a duplicate.
Provide your synopsis and a cover letter containing your full contact information.

Thanks for considering LDP and Ca$h Presents.

NEW RELEASES

BLOODLINE OF A SAVAGE 1&2
THESE VICIOUS STREETS 1&2
RELENTLESS GOON
RELENTLESS GOON 2
BY PRINCE A. TAUHID

THE BUTTERFLY MAFIA 1-3
BY FUMIYA PAYNE

A THUG'S STREET PRINCESS 1&2
BY MEESHA

CITY OF SMOKE 2
BY MOLOTTI

STEPPERS 1,2&3
THE REAL BADDIES OF CHI-RAQ
BY KING RIO

THE LANE 1&2
BY KEN-KEN SPENCE

THUG OF SPADES 1&2
LOVE IN THE TRENCHES 2
CORNER BOYS
BY COREY ROBINSON

TIL DEATH 3

GET IT IN SLUGS 2 | B. STALL

BY ARYANNA

THE BIRTH OF A GANGSTER 4
BY DELMONT PLAYER

PRODUCT OF THE STREETS 1&2
BY DEMOND "MONEY" ANDERSON

NO TIME FOR ERROR
BY KEESE

MONEY HUNGRY DEMONS
BY TRANAY ADAMS

Coming Soon from Lock Down Publications/Ca$h Presents

IF YOU CROSS ME ONCE 6
ANGEL V
By Anthony Fields

IMMA DIE BOUT MINE 5
By Aryanna

A THUGS STREET PRINCESS 3
By Meesha

PRODUCT OF THE STREETS 3
By Demond Money Anderson

CORNER BOYS 2
By Corey Robinson

THE MURDER QUEENS 6&7
By Michael Gallon

CITY OF SMOKE 3
By Molotti

CONFESSIONS OF A DOPE BOY
By Nicholas Lock

THA TAKEOVER
By Keith Chandler

BETRAYAL OF A G 2
By Ray Vinci

CRIME BOSS
By Playa Ray

Available Now

RESTRAINING ORDER 1 & 2
By **CA$H & Coffee**

LOVE KNOWS NO BOUNDARIES 1-3
By **Coffee**

RAISED AS A GOON I, II, III & IV
BRED BY THE SLUMS I, II, III
BLAST FOR ME I & II
ROTTEN TO THE CORE I II III
A BRONX TALE I, II, III
DUFFLE BAG CARTEL I II III IV V VI
HEARTLESS GOON I II III IV V
A SAVAGE DOPEBOY I II
DRUG LORDS I II III
CUTTHROAT MAFIA I II
KING OF THE TRENCHES
By **Ghost**

LAY IT DOWN I & II
LAST OF A DYING BREED I II
BLOOD STAINS OF A SHOTTA I & II III
By **Jamaica**

LOYAL TO THE GAME I II III
LIFE OF SIN I, II III
By **TJ & Jelissa**

GET IT IN SLUGS 2 | B. STALL

IF LOVING HIM IS WRONG...I & II
LOVE ME EVEN WHEN IT HURTS I II III
By **Jelissa**

PUSH IT TO THE LIMIT
By **Bre' Hayes**

BLOODY COMMAS I & II
SKI MASK CARTEL I, II & III
KING OF NEW YORK I II, III IV V
RISE TO POWER I II III
COKE KINGS I II III IV V
BORN HEARTLESS I II III IV
KING OF THE TRAP I II
By **T.J. Edwards**

WHEN THE STREETS CLAP BACK I & II III
THE HEART OF A SAVAGE I II III IV
MONEY MAFIA I II
LOYAL TO THE SOIL I II III
By **Jibril Williams**

A DISTINGUISHED THUG STOLE MY HEART I II & III
LOVE SHOULDN'T HURT I II III IV
RENEGADE BOYS 1-4
PAID IN KARMA 1-3
SAVAGE STORMS 1-3
AN UNFORESEEN LOVE 1-3
BABY, I'M WINTERTIME COLD 1-3
A THUG'S STREET PRINCESS 1&2
By **Meesha**

A GANGSTER'S CODE 1-3
A GANGSTER'S SYN 1-3
THE SAVAGE LIFE 1-3
CHAINED TO THE STREETS 1-3
BLOOD ON THE MONEY 1-3
A GANGSTA'S PAIN 1-3

GET IT IN SLUGS 2 | B. STALL

BEAUTIFUL LIES AND UGLY TRUTHS
CHURCH IN THESE STREETS
By **J-Blunt**

CUM FOR ME 1-8
An LDP Erotica Collaboration

BLOOD OF A BOSS 1-5
SHADOWS OF THE GAME
TRAP BASTARD
By **Askari**

THE STREETS BLEED MURDER 1-3
THE HEART OF A GANGSTA 1-3
By **Jerry Jackson**

WHEN A GOOD GIRL GOES BAD
By **Adrienne**

THE COST OF LOYALTY 1-3
By **Kweli**

BRIDE OF A HUSTLA 1-3
THE FETTI GIRLS 1-3
CORRUPTED BY A GANGSTA 1-4
BLINDED BY HIS LOVE
THE PRICE YOU PAY FOR LOVE 1-3
DOPE GIRL MAGIC 1-3
By **Destiny Skai**

A KINGPIN'S AMBITION
A KINGPIN'S AMBITION II
I MURDER FOR THE DOUGH
By **Ambitious**

TRUE SAVAGE 1-7
DOPE BOY MAGIC 1-3
MIDNIGHT CARTEL 1-3

GET IT IN SLUGS 2 | B. STALL

CITY OF KINGZ 1&2
NIGHTMARE ON SILENT AVE
THE PLUG OF LIL MEXICO 1&2
CLASSIC CITY
By **Chris Green**

A GANGSTER'S REVENGE 1-4
THE BOSS MAN'S DAUGHTERS 1-5
A SAVAGE LOVE 1&2
BAE BELONGS TO ME 1&2
A HUSTLER'S DECEIT 1-3
WHAT BAD BITCHES DO 1-3
SOUL OF A MONSTER 1-3
KILL ZONE
A DOPE BOY'S QUEEN 1-3
TIL DEATH 1-3
IMMA DIE BOUT MINE 1-4
By **Aryanna**

A DOPEBOY'S PRAYER
By **Eddie "Wolf" Lee**

THE KING CARTEL 1-3
By **Frank Gresham**

THESE NIGGAS AIN'T LOYAL 1-3
By **Nikki Tee**

GANGSTA SHYT 1-3
By **CATO**

THE ULTIMATE BETRAYAL
By **Phoenix**

BOSS'N UP 1-3
By **Royal Nicole**

GET IT IN SLUGS 2 | B. STALL

I LOVE YOU TO DEATH
By **Destiny J**

I RIDE FOR MY HITTA
I STILL RIDE FOR MY HITTA
By **Misty Holt**

LOVE & CHASIN' PAPER
By **Qay Crockett**

TO DIE IN VAIN
SINS OF A HUSTLA
By **ASAD**

BROOKLYN HUSTLAZ
By **Boogsy Morina**

BROOKLYN ON LOCK 1 & 2
By **Sonovia**

GANGSTA CITY
By **Teddy Duke**

A DRUG KING AND HIS DIAMOND 1-3
A DOPEMAN'S RICHES
HER MAN, MINE'S TOO 1&2
CASH MONEY HO'S
THE WIFEY I USED TO BE 1&2
PRETTY GIRLS DO NASTY THINGS
By **Nicole Goosby**

LIPSTICK KILLAH 1-3
CRIME OF PASSION 1-3
FRIEND OR FOE 1-3
By **Mimi**

TRAPHOUSE KING 1-3
KINGPIN KILLAZ 1-3
STREET KINGS 1&2

GET IT IN SLUGS 2 | B. STALL

PAID IN BLOOD 1&2
CARTEL KILLAZ 1-3
DOPE GODS 1&2
By **Hood Rich**

THE STREETS ARE CALLING
By **Duquie Wilson**

STEADY MOBBN' 1-3
THE STREETS STAINED MY SOUL 1-3
By **Marcellus Allen**

WHO SHOT YA 1-3
SON OF A DOPE FIEND 1-4
HEAVEN GOT A GHETTO 1&2
SKI MASK MONEY 1&2
By **Renta**

GORILLAZ IN THE BAY 1-4
TEARS OF A GANGSTA 1/&2
3X KRAZY 1&2
STRAIGHT BEAST MODE 1&2
By **DE'KARI**

TRIGGADALE 1-3
MURDA WAS THE CASE 1-3
By **Elijah R. Freeman**

SLAUGHTER GANG 1-3
RUTHLESS HEART 1-3
By **Willie Slaughter**

GOD BLESS THE TRAPPERS 1-3
THESE SCANDALOUS STREETS 1-3
FEAR MY GANGSTA 1-5
THESE STREETS DON'T LOVE NOBODY 1-2
BURY ME A G 1-5
A GANGSTA'S EMPIRE 1-4
THE DOPEMAN'S BODYGAURD 1&2

GET IT IN SLUGS 2 | B. STALL

THE REALEST KILLAZ 1-3
THE LAST OF THE OGS 1-3
By **Tranay Adams**

MARRIED TO A BOSS 1-3
By **Destiny Skai & Chris Green**

KINGZ OF THE GAME 1-7
CRIME BOSS 1-3
By **Playa Ray**

FUK SHYT
By **Blakk Diamond**

DON'T F#CK WITH MY HEART 1&2
By **Linnea**

ADDICTED TO THE DRAMA 1-3
IN THE ARM OF HIS BOSS
By **Jamila**

LOYALTY AIN'T PROMISED 1&2
By **Keith Williams**

YAYO 1-4
A SHOOTER'S AMBITION 1&2
BRED IN THE GAME
By **S. Allen**

TRAP GOD 1-3
RICH $AVAGE 1-3
MONEY IN THE GRAVE 1-3
CARTEL MONEY
By **Martell Troublesome Bolden**

FOREVER GANGSTA 1&2
GLOCKS ON SATIN SHEETS 1&2
By **Adrian Dulan**

TOE TAGZ 1-4
LEVELS TO THIS SHYT 1&2
IT'S JUST ME AND YOU
By **Ah'Million**

KINGPIN DREAMS 1-3
RAN OFF ON DA PLUG
By **Paper Boi Rari**

THE STREETS MADE ME 1-3
By **Larry D. Wright**

CONFESSIONS OF A GANGSTA 1-4
CONFESSIONS OF A JACKBOY 1-3
CONFESSIONS OF A HITMAN
By **Nicholas Lock**

I'M NOTHING WITHOUT HIS LOVE
SINS OF A THUG
TO THE THUG I LOVED BEFORE
A GANGSTA SAVED XMAS
IN A HUSTLER I TRUST
By **Monet Dragun**

QUIET MONEY 1-3
THUG LIFE 1-3
EXTENDED CLIP 1&2
A GANGSTA'S PARADISE
By **Trai'Quan**

CAUGHT UP IN THE LIFE 1-3
THE STREETS NEVER LET GO 1-3
By **Robert Baptiste**

NEW TO THE GAME 1-3
MONEY, MURDER & MEMORIES 1-3
By **Malik D. Rice**

CREAM 2-3
THE STREETS WILL TALK
By **Yolanda Moore**

THE STREETS WILL NEVER CLOSE 1-3
By **K'ajji**

LIFE OF A SAVAGE 1-4
A GANGSTA'S QUR'AN 1-4
MURDA SEASON 1-3
GANGLAND CARTEL 1-3
CHI'RAQ GANGSTAS 1-4
KILLERS ON ELM STREET 1-3
JACK BOYZ N DA BRONX 1-3
A DOPEBOY'S DREAM 1-3
JACK BOYS VS DOPE BOYS 1-3
COKE GIRLZ
COKE BOYS
SOSA GANG 1&2
BRONX SAVAGES
BODYMORE KINGPINS
BLOOD OF A GOON
By **Romell Tukes**

CONCRETE KILLA 1-3
VICIOUS LOYALTY 1-3
By **Kingpen**

THE ULTIMATE SACRIFICE 1-6
KHADIFI
IF YOU CROSS ME ONCE 1-3
ANGEL 1-4
IN THE BLINK OF AN EYE
By **Anthony Fields**

THE LIFE OF A HOOD STAR
By **Ca$h & Rashia Wilson**

GET IT IN SLUGS 2 | B. STALL

NIGHTMARES OF A HUSTLA 1-3
BLOOD AND GAMES 1&2
By **King Dream**

GHOST MOB
By **Stilloan Robinson**

HARD AND RUTHLESS 1&2
MOB TOWN 251
THE BILLIONAIRE BENTLEYS 1-3
REAL G'S MOVE IN SILENCE
By **Von Diesel**

MOB TIES 1-7
SOUL OF A HUSTLER, HEART OF A KILLER 1-3
GORILLAZ IN THE TRENCHES
By **SayNoMore**

BODYMORE MURDERLAND 1-3
THE BIRTH OF A GANGSTER 1-4
By **Delmont Player**

FOR THE LOVE OF A BOSS 1&2
By **C. D. Blue**

KILLA KOUNTY 1-5
By **Khufu**

MOBBED UP 1-4
THE BRICK MAN 1-5
THE COCAINE PRINCESS 1-10
STEPPERS 1-3
SUPER GREMLIN 1-4
By **King Rio**

MONEY GAME 1&2
By **Smoove Dolla**

GET IT IN SLUGS 2 | B. STALL

A GANGSTA'S KARMA 1-4
By **FLAME**

KING OF THE TRENCHES 1-3
By **GHOST & TRANAY ADAMS**

QUEEN OF THE ZOO 1&2
By **Black Migo**

GRIMEY WAYS 1-3
BETRAYAL OF A G
By **Ray Vinci**

XMAS WITH AN ATL SHOOTER
By **Ca$h & Destiny Skai**

KING KILLA 1&2
By **Vincent "Vitto" Holloway**

BETRAYAL OF A THUG 1&2
By **Fre$h**

THE MURDER QUEENS 1-5
By **Michael Gallon**

FOR THE LOVE OF BLOOD 1-4
By **Jamel Mitchell**

HOOD CONSIGLIERE 1&2
NO TIME FOR ERROR
By **Keese**

PROTÉGÉ OF A LEGEND 1&2
LOVE IN THE TRENCHES 1&2
By **Corey Robinson**

THE PLUG'S RUTHLESS DAUGHTER
By **Tony Daniels**

GET IT IN SLUGS 2 | B. STALL

BORN IN THE GRAVE 1-3
CRIME PAYS
By **Self Made Tay**

MOAN IN MY MOUTH
By **XTASY**

TORN BETWEEN A GANGSTER AND A GENTLEMAN
By **J-BLUNT & Miss Kim**

LOYALTY IS EVERYTHING 1-3
CITY OF SMOKE 1&2
By **Molotti**

HERE TODAY GONE TOMORROW 1&2
By **Fly Rock**

WOMEN LIE MEN LIE 1-4
FIFTY SHADES OF SNOW 1-3
STACK BEFORE YOU SPLURGE
GIRLS FALL LIKE DOMINOES
NAÏVE TO THE STREETS
By **ROY MILLIGAN**

PILLOW PRINCESS
By **S. Hawkins**

THE BUTTERFLY MAFIA 1-3
SALUTE MY SAVAGERY 1&2
By **Fumiya Payne**

THE LANE 1&2
By Ken-Ken Spence

THE PUSSY TRAP 1-5
By **Nene Capri**

DIRTY DNA

By **Blaque**

SANCTIFIED AND HORNY
by **XTASY**

BOOKS BY LDP'S CEO, CA$H

TRUST IN NO MAN
TRUST IN NO MAN 2
TRUST IN NO MAN 3
BONDED BY BLOOD
SHORTY GOT A THUG
THUGS CRY
THUGS CRY 2
THUGS CRY 3
TRUST NO BITCH
TRUST NO BITCH 2
TRUST NO BITCH 3
TIL MY CASKET DROPS
RESTRAINING ORDER
RESTRAINING ORDER 2
IN LOVE WITH A CONVICT
LIFE OF A HOOD STAR
XMAS WITH AN ATL SHOOTER

www.ingramcontent.com/pod-product-compliance
Lightning Source LLC
Chambersburg PA
CBHW070446260626
47161CB00004B/1223